CHRISTOPHER GAFFNEY

Monaguillos

Bless Me Father For I Am Awkward

First edition

ISBN: 979-8-218-85883-4

This book was professionally typeset on Reedsy.
Find out more at reedsy.com

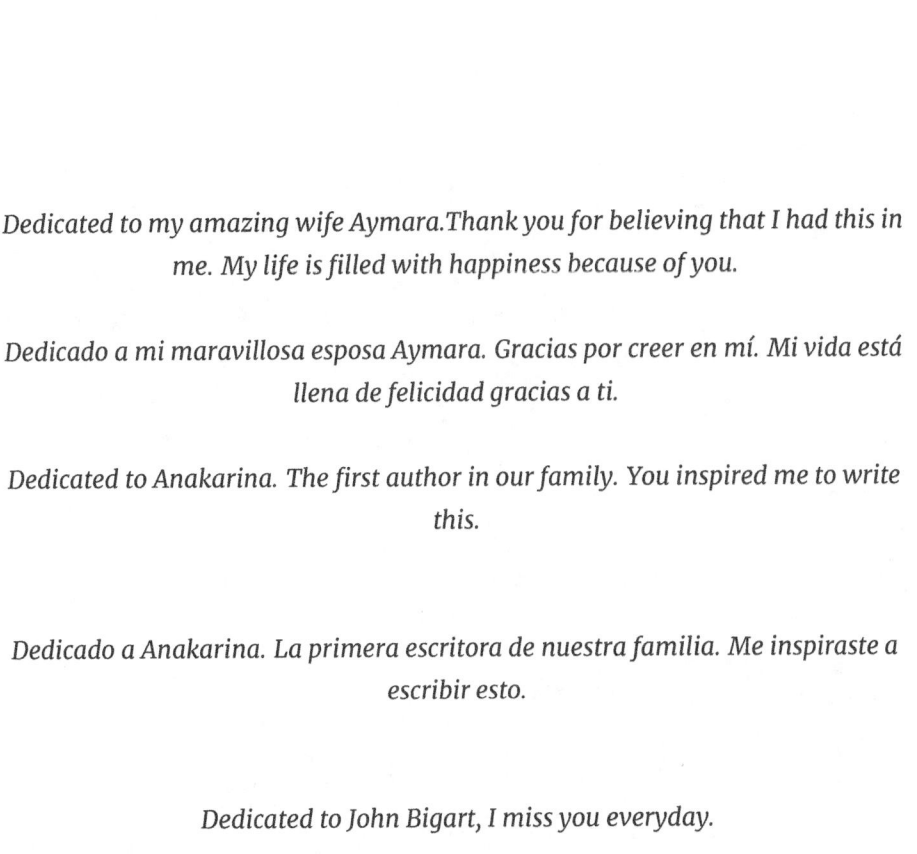

Dedicated to my amazing wife Aymara.Thank you for believing that I had this in me. My life is filled with happiness because of you.

Dedicado a mi maravillosa esposa Aymara. Gracias por creer en mí. Mi vida está llena de felicidad gracias a ti.

Dedicated to Anakarina. The first author in our family. You inspired me to write this.

Dedicado a Anakarina. La primera escritora de nuestra familia. Me inspiraste a escribir esto.

Dedicated to John Bigart, I miss you everyday.

Christopher Gaffney

Contents

1

The Storage Unit

Mara paired her jeans with her "Cyndi Lauper" shoes for a brilliant look for the flight from Texas to Florida. After landing in Miami, they proceeded from the airport to a storage unit. Mara still wore the warm clothes she had on when she boarded the flight from Texas, where an atypical chill gripped the air. Hence, the warm "Cyndi Lauper" shoes. That year, the couple, married for 3 years, were in Miami to get an original copy of Chris's birth certificate. They needed it for Mara's upcoming interview with immigration officials concerning her impending US citizenship quest. What they were finding instead were forgotten treasures of Chris's youth. Never comfortable discussing his childhood or anything in the past tense, Chris tried to redirect Mara to the task at hand, to find the birth certificate.

"Mara- eyes on the prize, focus... let's find the birth certificate first, then we can look for other stuff," Chris said. Mara ignored him. Chris remained patient, in part, because he knew his wife was curious about how her husband came to be.

In the storage building on US 1 near Ponce De Leon Blvd, the musty smell surrounded them, old memories lingering in the air like ghosts from the past. Hoping to introduce some light to the space, Chris propped the door open with some boxes. He found one heavy box that would keep the door from closing.

With a playful smile, she nudged her husband, her voice laced with excitement. "¡Ay!" Mara wrinkled her nose, swiping a finger across a box to reveal a layer of grime underneath. She chuckled, her Venezuelan accent seasoning the air as she cried, "Ay, Dios mío, ¿qué tenemos aquí? Dusting it off, she was surprised and excitedly said, "Mira, check this out." Chris knelt, eyes glued to the phone. The device seemed like a relic from a distant past. Its sturdy frame and coiled cord whisper tales of long-forgotten conversations. The faint light enhanced her beauty and highlighted her curious look. Chris felt a surge of affection for her, grateful for her unwavering interest in his past. He cradled the worn edges of the phone, a flood of memories washing over him.

Chris: "This phone is older than I am."

Mara: "Ha ha.... it is old, we had one like it in our house in Venezuela."

Chris: "I am not exaggerating; I think this phone is older than me. Chris said, "I think about the calls made on that phone." The receiver's color was no longer white, but yellow. Then it hit him; he remembered a particular phone call he made in 10th grade. The memory brought a hint of a smile to his face. Mara knew her husband and recognized the beginnings of that smile. She also knew there was no chance he would volunteer what had brought that smile, so she playfully asked him.

"Cuentame!!!! Tell me, tell me the phone calls you made with this phone. Maybe you called muchas chicas??"

His face, red with embarrassment, said. "OK, one story, that's all you're gonna get."

***

Grace was more than just a crush. She wasn't the typical Catholic schoolgirl giggling through adolescent braces. She seemed more controlled, graceful, and mature. She certainly caught my attention. I was way behind my classmates in most things social. Especially girls.

My romantic awakening followed the same delayed timeline. My all-boys Catholic high school didn't make things happen any faster. Though not the monastery-like prison outsiders might imagine, it shielded me from certain realities.

The way I imagined teenage boys transforming into peacocks the moment girls enter the room. Without "hens" in our henhouse, we had no reason to fluff our feathers or crow at dawn. I'd estimate that about 90% of adolescent male foolishness exists to capture female attention.

Jesuit Prep and its sister school, St. Mary's Academy, often collaborated on events. Once a month, the two schools would have special masses together. The only thing I liked about the combined mass was hearing the cello. I loved the sweet yet haunting sounds of those strings filling the walls and rafters of St. Francis of Assisi, the church that hosted our combined mass and one of the two churches that shaped my young life. With my Jesuit Prep brethren on one side of the church, while the St. Mary's girls occupied the other side of the central aisle. Blazers and ties lined the left section, while plaid skirts and high socks filled the section to the right.

And in the middle sits the cello, its beautiful sounds, welcoming the blazers and plaid skirts in the church. My focus centered on the cello. I'm no fan of classical music, but the cello transfixed me. But in actuality it wasn't the cello it was the CELLIST that transfixed me.

I knew her name was Grace, I knew this because whenever the priest began Mass, he also said,

"Thank you, Grace...... as always- beautiful."

To which I always agreed. Grace was a petite girl. Dark blonde hair and brown eyes, a contrast from what I was accustomed to seeing among the daughters of the Cuban-American upper crust of Miami society. On occasion, I would see someone with blonde hair and blue eyes. Or brown eyes with black hair, or another dark color. The combination of blonde hair/brown eyes was unique. The contrast looked good on her.

I wanted to approach Grace, speak to her. But insecurities and doubts held me back, chaining me to my seat in the sea of blazers and ties. What could I, a shy and awkward boy, offer someone as enchanting as her? However, luck was on my side. She knew who I was, sort of.

The two schools shared other activities, including after-school ventures such as sports, cheerleading, and other extracurricular activities. The Jesuit brothers and Dominican nuns sought chances for students from each school to meet. St. Mary's girls were cheerleaders for the sports of both schools, and the two schools also had a combined marching band. I'm told the trips the marching band took were legendary.

Grace played in the marching band, and I played on Jesuit's football team; therefore, she knew me. Sports provided me with my only authentic social outlet. I wasn't a star on the football team, but I was a skillful player and as a recognized athlete she knew who I was, and that was my "in". I could never just go up to a girl and start talking; I couldn't go in "cold." So at least we did have some common ground. But I needed to act. Luckily for me, as the school year progressed, my courage grew as well. Well, progression is a relative term. My progression consisted of smiling and nodding at her from my seat during Mass. I always waited until between songs to smile at the blond-haired, brown-eyed cellist.

From there, I would progress to saying hello. It was not just a usual hello; it was a hello that only I could deliver. An individual with both shyness and cowardice could perform this action. You see, a typical high school junior, who was my age, would say hello differently. They could approach a high school junior, Grace's age, and say, "Hi, Grace, how are you?" Another approach common for the adolescent male may be to say hello by flirting and drawing attention to themselves. I did not, and I could not subscribe to either approach. My approach was different, sadder, desperate.

I would synchronize my exit from St. Francis of Assisi's foyer with hers. After mass ended, everyone gathered to board their school's buses back to their campuses. This procession, as judged by the blazer/ ties and plaid skirts/ white socks, was the best and most worthwhile section of the mass. It was all because it was a chance to interact with students of the opposite sex. Even if it lasted only 10 minutes. I'm sure those 10 minutes would form suitable content for early nature programs on cable television. "The courting rituals of young humans"

For the first time in my life, I would become part of this timeless courting ritual; all I had to do was execute perfect timing. Even if it meant waiting until the entire church emptied, my aim was to create a "bump in" or chance meeting. A meeting where we both occupied the same space. Brilliant approach, pathetic too. But as an 11th grader, pathetic was my middle name. So, in these "bump-ins", I still didn't progress much past the smile at her stage. I did, however, summon the courage to say, albeit clumsily, "hello"... not "Hello Grace, my name is Chris" or even a simple

"Hi Grace".... I just uttered "hello." Smooth.

Slow and sure wins the race. Well, in my case, I hadn't even gotten that far. After post-mass bump-ins and post-cello solo smiles, I was still waiting for my moment, perhaps Christmas vacation. I had plenty of time. Haha... At this pace, I will have the courage to approach her around my 40th birthday. Procrastination was also my middle name.

However, Catholic school intervened; was it divine intervention? Someone had to intervene; it would not be me. Haha. Father Ramirez, St. Francis's head priest, approached me after one mass and asked me if I could do some of the mass's scripture readings. We always alternated a Jesuit Prep boy and a St. Mary's girl for the readings. Father Ramirez's request surprised me. Me, doing the scripture readings during Mass? It seemed like a divine intervention, a push in the right direction. Maybe this was the nudge I needed to break my shell and talk to Grace.

TThe following Wednesday, I stood at the lectern, scanning the pews for Grace's familiar face. As I read the scripture, my voice wavered, but I pushed through, determined to make an impression. After the Mass ended, Father Ramirez congratulated me on a job well done.

Heart pounding in my chest, I gathered my courage and made my way towards Grace. That was it, that precise instant I had expected. I walked towards her, and she faced me with a warm smile. "Hi," her eyes lit up in recognition. But I still lacked the courage to follow up. I scurried to my bus to take me back to school. I considered that a significant victory. I was in!!

The next few Wednesday Masses became something I looked forward to each week. All the other ties/sport jackets and plaid skirts/white socks filed into their seats in the church. The other "performers" and I would meet in the sacristy to prepare to take part in the mass, including altar boys (Monaguillos), servers, and Grace and me. We donned the familiar cassocks and gowns. A throwback to my Monaguillo days. I loved that time because it created an opportunity to interact with my favorite cellist. Divine intervention forced Grace and me together; otherwise, I would never have found myself with her. We even found things to talk about. We talked about what our futures would look like.

Chris: "I'm not sure what I want to do...But I know what I don't want to do. "

Grace: "I don't get it...what don't you want to do?"

Chris: "I don't want to do that?!"

I pointed with my face from my chair in the sacristy toward Fr. Ramirez.

Chris: "I don't want to be a priest. "

Grace laughed; she didn't understand the seriousness of what I had just said. I laughed and told her that when I was younger, I aspired to be a priest. Realizing Grace wasn't laughing at the idea of wanting to be a priest, I thought it was endearing. She was impressed, and that made me feel less like an outcast. I had gone so long feeling I had to project an image of "being cool" that I had punched out of my mind my early desire to be a priest. Grace had a kind way of making me and others feel good about ourselves.

Grace: "You would've been an excellent priest; you're kind... but you are way too cute."

We both laughed at that one. The redness of my blush punctuated my laugh. Grace wasn't shy. That was my first impression. Although quiet, she wasn't shy. She selected her words with care. Also, she put limitations on them.

Each week, we became a little closer. I learned Grace's (grace?) stemmed beyond her cello-playing talent. She was the eldest girl in her family. She had 3 younger sisters. Her parents depended on her to help with the little ones. That brings maturity. She differed from the other St Mary's girls in that way. She was a working-class girl in a working-class family. Other girls attending St. Mary's had privileges. So, she and I stood out from the crowd because of that.

As the school year progressed and the calendar approached May, I finally made a serious move. I called her on the phone. Landlines were my solace; no face-to-face meetings were needed. If I were rejected, it would be better not to have to look at the person while she did it.

Grace's number was easy to find. Remember the white pages? The phone book? Finding the bravery to approach her remained the only barrier. To make that call, I couldn't delay it anymore. Even though I tried. My original plan was to call Grace at 7:00pm. I figured her family dinner time would have been finished by then. But when 7pm came, my father was still in the kitchen washing dishes. That was his "chore". But I'm sure our human dishwasher would feel far more awkward than I would. Genetics in action, for sure, I inherited my social skills from my father. So, Dad still washing the dishes provided some relief for me. I was relieved to be able to delay it some more.

Okay, I thought, I'll call her when Dad is out of the kitchen, and then no one will be within listening distance. At 7:15 pm, my heart quickened, and I scrambled for a way to postpone my call again. So, I adapted the "snooze button" approach. Alarm goes off in the morning? Hit the snooze button, buy yourself 15 more minutes. The same concept applies here. Hit the snooze button and delay making a fool of yourself by getting rejected by a girl for a few more minutes. Whew... sweet <u>relief</u>, so 7:15pm became 7:30pm, which of course turned into 7:45pm.

The courage to call didn't appear until 8:15 p.m.... I dialed her number, the sound of each ring echoing in my ear. My heart raced as I waited for her to answer, my palms sweaty and my throat dry. After what seemed like an eternity, I heard her voice on the other end of the line.

"Hello?" she asked, her voice melodic and sweet, making me shiver.

"Hello, Grace," I said, my voice breaking as I stammered, "It's Chris from Jesuit Prep."

I feared the worst following the silence. Maybe Grace didn't remember me, or perhaps she wondered why I called her out of the blue. But then, to my surprise and relief, she responded.

"Chris, hey!" I passed the first checkpoint. She didn't reject me. The first conversation was pleasant. On a rare occasion during my youthful existence, I felt at ease. We talked a lot. She had a unique voice, raspy but soft. The voice invited easy conversation. Disarming, sweet, and humble. Grace differed from the typical St Mary's girl. Grace didn't speak the same rhythm as they did. That was a relief, because I had met enough of them. The St Mary's girl archetype spoke too strongly and too fast. Voices that screamed for attention, and not in a good way.

The attention that screamed, "Look at me". When I say, "Look at me", I'm telling you to buy me a Cartier watch, Daddy.

Grace's voice was distinct. She spoke in controlled sentences. Avoiding attention rather than craving it. Her quiet confidence was clear — a feat difficult to achieve. I even struggled to hear her through our old house phone's tiny speaker. We spoke for 2 hours. We talked so much that I received quizzical looks from both my brother and my father. Thank goodness my mother wasn't home. She worked nights. She would quiz me about the mysterious individual I was conversing with. For sure, she would have known it wasn't my best friend, Barnsy, on the phone with me. We never spoke on the phone that long, and if we had, we would have punctuated it with laughter. This was different, and I didn't want anyone in my house to offer their opinions on who or why I tied up the phone for 2 hours. I knew it was 2 hours because I was trying to muster up the courage to even dial the number at first. As I hung up, I looked at the clock; it was 10:20 p.m.

The phone in my childhood home was in the kitchen, the highest-traffic room in the entire house. The telephone cord allowed it to extend to the pantry entrance, offering privacy. But that night, I chose not to opt for privacy for fear that it would create more scrutiny. If I had dared to take the phone receiver and its corresponding cord and close the pantry stair door behind me, I would have invited ridicule. My brother Jon would have terrorized me. My father would have been embarrassed enough for both me and him. So, I didn't dare. I placed a phone call with inspiration... with confidence... but also with my shoulders slumped forward and my voice softer than a whisper. That tiny kitchen corner enclosed my body, cocoon-like. I spoke so that the KGB and MI5 would never have heard me. But somehow, Grace could understand me.. Easy, smooth, and comfortable. I couldn't wait to do it again.

The very next Wednesday Mass, I was full of courage (and also fear). It was the last Mass of that school year, so I knew that unless I did something, I would not see Grace until the next school year began. The year's last Mass was a stripped-down, no-frills affair. Grace did not play the cello, nor did I present a scripture reading. So, both Grace and I had to sit in our assigned areas with that aisle between us. That aisle felt like a castle's moat. Only, instead of containing alligators in it, this one had nuns!! These nuns were twice as effective and ten times scarier than any alligator. No tie/blazer was getting by them if they tried to cross to where the plaid skirts/white socks were found. No one dared to try.

Except me.

With the Mass ending, fear overtook. I might not see Grace until August. I traversed the aisle. Crossing the nun-guarded moat didn't bother me, despite the other St. Mary's girls chuckling. I crossed, intending to ask Grace out on a date. Showing silent admiration and not the slightest bit of embarrassment, Grace kept eye contact with me the whole time, and when I said the words:

Chris: "Would you like to go on a date with me?" She spoke sincerely and with style. Grace said, "Yes, I would love that."

***

2

Cello Girl

She watched him, eyes fixed on some distant, imagined point beyond her shoulder. He looked suddenly older and simultaneously very young, like a schoolboy waiting for the teacher's approval. Mara felt a fierce love for him, the kind that made her want to both cradle and tease him. She let her hand settle gently on his and said nothing for a while.

She thought about how rarely he talked about his youth, how the stories she knew of his family and childhood were scattered and incomplete, like pieces of a puzzle that didn't always fit. There was the father, a former boxer and silent; the mother, working nights, navigating a house full of men. The brothers are both a lot older. He was so old that he felt like an only child. There were churches and schools, phone calls and nuns, all filtered through that dry, self-deprecating humor that was both his shield and his armor. Sometimes Mara wondered if the real Chris—the raw, unedited Chris—existed anywhere outside of these rare, late-night anecdotes.

She realized, too, how hard it must be for him to share this memory. He had always been the immigrant in his own family, the one who never quite learned the language of belonging. She, on the other hand, was an immigrant in the literal sense. It was almost funny, the way their roles mirrored each other: both outsiders, both experts in the art of navigating foreign landscapes. Maybe that was why they had found each other, why their marriage worked in its patchwork way.

Mara squeezed his hand, and when she spoke, her accent thickened deliberately, the way it did when she wanted to remind him that she was not from here, that she had her own country of memories and ghosts.

"You know, Chris," she said, "I think you are not so different from me. We both come from places we don't return to."

She paused, searching his face for a sign that her words had landed, that he heard her.

"In Venezuela," she said, "we used to joke that......." She did not finish the joke. She probably thought he wouldn't like it, so she kept it in. But she couldn't resist poking at least a little fun. At that moment, Chris looked up at her, his blue eyes lighter now, the storytelling haze replaced by a kind of gratitude. He shrugged, let out a laugh, and Mara felt the tension in the room ease.

"So," she said, "did you ever go out with Grace? The cello girl?"

His cheeks colored in the familiar boyish way, and Mara laughed out loud.

"Do you have to know?" Chris asked.

"Claro que si!!....cuentame" Mara said.

"You won't let it go, will you?". Chris squirmed in his makeshift chair inside the storage unit as it suddenly started to warm up. He shifted as he sighed a simple.

"OK" ...." It didn't end well."

"Obviously, you are married to me," Mara said through her laughter.

"NO!, Chris said, I told only one story........besides, we are here to find the birth certificate." Chris knew Mara was unsatisfied; the look she gave him indicated she needed closure about Grace. All she said was;

"Continua"

Chris said, "Ayy Dios here we go" ....Chris glanced at Mara, a small smile playing on his lips as she teased him about being married to her. He shook his head slightly, his blue eyes reflecting a mix of fondness and exasperation. "You never miss a chance, do you?" he mused, his voice carrying a hint of amusement.

As he looked around the storage unit, Chris noticed the dust particles swirling in a beam of light that sneaked through a crack in the door. The air felt stale, making him wrinkle his nose involuntarily. He shifted in his seat, feeling the edges of a cardboard box dig into his back. He eyes that crack in the door, wishing he were small enough to escape through it and be freed from telling this story...Nonetheless, he continued.... "You're doing it... You're telling me the story in flashback style", joked Mara.

***

Salzedo St. felt like a tank was rolling down it.

Silver on top and wood panels along the sides. It was a majestic mode of transportation, motoring towards my house. We are, of course, talking about the Oldsmobile Vista Cruiser station wagon, 1972 edition. The early evening's setting sun glistened off this mean machine. Butterflies were building in my stomach, and I could see the massive vehicle more clearly as it got closer. I thought to myself, and I even said to myself.

"I think this is her. "

The Oldsmobile Vista Cruiser station Wagon, 1972 model, dropped anchor in the driveway of my parents' house. As the car approached, terror overcame me. Worry gnawed at me, leaving me restless. I waited in the only room in our house that faced the front. From that vantage point, I had a view of any car approaching our house. I stared out the window, waiting. Like a puppy. The way our dachshund puppy, "Fraulein," used to act when it was time for my father to get home from work. When she saw the car pull in the driveway, she would wag her tail and bound off towards the door, all excited to greet my father. At this moment, I was the puppy waiting for Grace. My middle name was Fraulein.

When I saw that chariot, that station wagon that could only be a product of Detroit, I ran from the kitchen window to the bathroom. I had to do a quick hair check. The mirror confirmed I was presentable. It lied. Remembering my manners, or more accurately, displaying my impatience, I opened the front door. I went outside to greet that spaceship of a car. Its front passenger door made a loud, painful-sounding creak as it opened. Before I even uttered words from my trembling mouth, a raspy but sweet voice beat me to it.

"Hi Chris!"

"I found your house easily. "

Grace had a good sense of direction... check! Another tick in the plus column, I thought to myself. As if to save me from myself and perhaps to foreshadow future events, Grace had made a preemptive strike. She called me earlier that afternoon to ask if I wanted to have ice cream with her. I was dumbfounded. I didn't see that coming. So, of course, I agreed. Grace had a part-time job at Swensen's, an ice cream parlor/diner. She said she had to go there to pick up a paycheck and knew I lived nearby. She offered to pick me up, and we could grab an ice cream cone together. I don't think of this as a first date, as much as a pre-first date. Whatever it was, I was nervous and happy.

So, after Grace appeared from the Oldsmobile Vista Cruiser, I made my way from the front door towards her and the car. Much to my surprise, 3 little giggles and smiles also greeted me. In the middle seat of the world's biggest station were Grace's 3 little sisters, Teresa, aged 13, and 9-year-old twins Maria and Colleen. Including Grace, and of course excluding me, the cuteness factor in the car was on overload. Grace apologized for having to bring the peanut gallery. Telling me that for her to borrow the car, or in this case, the armored fortress of a station wagon, she had to include the little sisters. Clearly, I needed more girls to scrutinize me on my first interaction with the fairer sex on a romantic level. I was not ready for all the giggles.

Seeing Grace's three young sisters in the Vista Cruiser brought a chuckle from me. They were all staring at me with wide eyes, braces, and mischievous grins, enjoying the spectacle unfolding before them. Teresa, Maria, and Colleen were assessing me, deciding if I merited their sister's time.

Grace herself looked amused at the situation, as if she had expected this chaos all along. She introduced me to her sisters, who responded with a chorus of giggles and shy hellos. It was endearing in a chaotic sort of way.

On the way to Swensen's in the car, I felt a sense of joy. Grace's presence was comforting; her sisters' energy was infectious. The nervousness that had gripped me earlier faded away, replaced by excitement and anticipation.

I glanced over at Grace in the driver's seat of the massive prehistoric family truckster. It was as if the car had swallowed her whole and left only her hands on the wheel. Even so, this was a magnificent setting with a carload of fun and positive energy. Just what I needed to make me less nervous.

As we drove towards Swensen's, the sun dipping lower in the sky, I couldn't help but steal glances at Grace whenever I thought she wasn't looking. There was something about her that drew me in — a warmth and kindness that radiated from her very being. I wanted to learn more about her, to unravel the layers of complexity that I sensed lay beneath her controlled exterior. It wasn't shyness; she possessed a quiet quality mature for a 17-year-old, as we both were. We were both incoming seniors at our respective schools.

When we arrived at Swensen's, the girls tumbled out of the car, their excitement palpable. Grace led the way into the ice cream parlor, her hand brushing against mine as we walked side by side.

As we stepped inside Swensen's, a wave of sugary sweetness enveloped us, blending with the chatter and laughter of the other patrons. The girls rushed over to the display case, their eyes wide with wonder at the colorful array of ice cream flavors.

Grace glanced back at me, a mischievous twinkle in her eye. "What do you think, Chris? Feeling adventurous today?"

I chuckled, knowing full well what she meant. "Are you going to make me try some exotic, rainbow pecan walnut monstrosity?" I replied, matching her playful tone. The things we do for love. I was a vanilla man for ice cream, in no way adventurous.

Her fun poke at my simple tastes got a laugh from me, since I knew I preferred old favorites. Yet, in that moment of shared laughter and scoops of unconventional flavors, I found myself drawn not only to the sweetness of the frozen treats but also to the warmth emanating from Grace's mischievous gaze.

Teenage crushes are a changeable feeling, making normal people brave seekers of the impossible ideal. And as we indulged in frozen delights amidst chatter and laughter, I couldn't help but savor the irony of it all—finding joy in unexpected places, even if it meant straying from my comfort zone.

During adolescent play and family pleasure, a strong tie was formed. And amidst the chaos and contradictions, I found solace in the simple moments shared with Grace and her spirited entourage—a reminder that even amid uncertainty, there is always room for laughter. And Ice Cream

**

3

The Envelope

Awwwww que lindo!!!...... every one of these memories gets cuter...."
Que adorable!!!".

His wife's playful comment brings him back to the present, and he can't help but smile at her teasing tone. Together, they continue to sift through the boxes, each item unearthing a different piece of their shared history. As Chris's story faded, Mara peeled back the yellowed plastic covering the album in her lap. Black and white faces stared up at her—solemn children trapped in their First Communion garb. Row after row of girls in lace-trimmed white, boys drowning in dark cassocks. Her fingertips skimmed across each glossy page, searching for a familiar face among the strangers. Then she found him—young, serious, his expression tight with discomfort. And just behind him, another boy with cheeks flushed dark even in monochrome, lips pressed together against escaping laughter.

"Look at your face!" Mara said, unable to hold her joy.

"Sooo intense! So cute!!" ..." Who are the other 2 Monaguillos behind you?" she asked.

"They look like they are laughing.... but you look so serious"

"That is Jon, my brother, and John, my childhood best friend", Chris answered.

"Do you remember that picture? Serious little boy."

"I remember, yes..... But the birth certificate won't be in a photo album. My mother would have put it with other important documents. Keep looking". Chris had to remind Mara why they were in the storage unit.

She didn't. Mara ignored him as she looked at the old photo.

"Mara, we need to find that document. If we don't find this document soon, things could get complicated."

"Yes, I know, but relax," was Mara's reply. Chris went on to explain, "I think it's best if we find it before 5pm. If it gets close to that and we don't find it, we should go to the courthouse."

"We have time, let's keep looking here, I'm having fun finding these old things". Chris relented, took a deep breath, and said the following;

"Church and school were a critical part of my upbringing; they shaped my morals, I suppose," Chris said. "Here is a good example".......

***

As if furious with me, the sun beat down on my neck, its relentless rays pricking my skin, while I hunched over the handlebars of my red Schwinn cruiser. The chipped paint gleamed under the fiery glare, and the worn rubber grips felt sticky in my palms. I pumped my legs desperately, the chain rattling in protest with every rotation. Ahead of me, Jon's sleek ten-speed Raleigh glided through the shimmering heat like a fish cutting through water. His bike was new, a birthday gift from Dad, and its glossy black frame seemed to taunt me with every effortless weave he made through the sparse Saturday morning traffic.

"Chris, get going!" Jon called over his shoulder, his voice carried by the faint breeze he created as he sped ahead. His grin was wide and teasing. "You're gonna make us later than we already are!"

Feeling each pedal stroke as punishment, I gritted my teeth and pushed harder. My thighs burned, and a sharp stitch formed in my side, but I refused to let Jon get too far ahead. "I'm trying! We don't all ride Raleighs!" I thought, though my words were likely lost in the rush of wind between us. I was tired of my old bike. It was a 1-speed. I wanted a 10-speed like the one Jon had. My friends were all getting 10-speeds, and I wanted one. I asked my parents for one, and they said no. But I kept asking, and eventually my parents said. "You want a bike? You can buy it yourself; you'd better save up some money."That sounded like a good idea to me. At least until I realized how hard it would be to both earn and save money. So I *did everything I could to earn the money: I mowed neighbors' lawns and washed cars and in between jobs I got my hands on the Montgomery Ward's catalog. I looked up the price and I was shocked. $65! That was a lot of money in the late 70's. But I had a good start, I had $30 in my savings account. I only needed $35 more. Watching Jon and his shiny 10 speed disappear in the distance in front of me was all the motivation I needed to earn that money.*

The humid air felt like wearing an extra layer of clothing. Our suburban world shimmered in the heat haze; pastel houses lined up along the streets like candy-colored sentinels guarding their immaculate green lawns. Sprinklers clicked, sending arcs of water across flowerbeds bursting with petunias and marigolds (at least I think that is what those flowers were). We whizzed past Mr. Hernandez standing by his driveway, hose in hand, as he watered his vibrant bougainvillea. He waved at us half-heatedly, but whiffed his head with disapproval when he noticed how fast we were going.

"You're gonna break your necks one day!" Though there was no real venom in his voice.

After laughing and popping onto the sidewalk, Jon briefly paused before returning to the street. "Tina!" — his nickname for me—"Try to keep up!"

"That's not my name!" I yelled. I also thought to myself, "Man, if I had a 10-speed, I would have no problem keeping up."

A beat-up Ford station wagon, having sputtered to a stop near the Venetian Pool, caused us to snap our heads up with its screech. The car door creaked open, and Mrs. Gonzalez appeared with her usual flair—tiny and birdlike, her cloud of cotton candy hair catching the sunlight like a halo. She wore a floral dress that looked vintage even when she bought it years ago, and her ever-present cigarette hung from her lips.

"Boys!" With mock exasperation and in her raspy smoker's voice, she said, "Late again," shaking her head. "Father Fred will tan your hides one day... .apurrate!!!!!!!!!....." Ya va....muchachos, ven aca"

While I rolled up more cautiously behind him, Jon stopped beside her car. "Morning, Mrs. Gonzalez," flashing her one of his charming smiles that could melt butter if he tried hard enough.

Before reaching into her oversized purse and pulling out a thick white envelope, Mrs. Gonzalez squinted at him. She held it out to me this time—her sharp eyes zeroing in on my sweaty face as if she'd already decided I was the more trustworthy of the two.

With a breath, she pressed the envelope into my reluctant hand. "Take this for me, hijo." "Put it straight into the collection plate during mass, okay? Don't you go losing it now."

Because the envelope was too heavy for its size, I felt Jon's gaze on me as I held it.

"Uh... sure thing," I felt my throat was like sandpaper.

"Good boy," with a satisfied nod, Mrs. Gonzalez climbed back into her car and drove away, leaving a trail of exhaust smoke in the humid air.

"What do you think's in there? I hope it isn't money." When I said that, Jon shot back. "Of course it's money!"

Before putting the envelope in my pocket, I stared at it longer than needed. "Dunno," though my mind was already racing with possibilities—cash? A check? Something else? I had a strong wish to give the envelope to Jon. I wanted to defer responsibility.

Jon smirked but didn't press further. "Better not lose it!" he called over his shoulder while pedaling away after hopping back onto his bike." Mrs. Gonzalez will haunt you forever if you do! La brujaaa!

With sweat running down our backs and breath coming in ragged gasps, we arrived at the church parking lot. The steeple loomed above us like a watchful eye peeking through swaying palm fronds

With arms crossed over his broad chest and a sour expression, Father Fred awaited our arrival at the entrance. Before Jon could launch into his usual excuses about flat tires or traffic, Father Fred stopped him.

"Save it," before unexpectedly thrusting an oversized cassock into my arms. "We're short a Monaguillo today—you'll have to do."

Frozen in horror, I watched Jon laugh next to me. I choked. The clothes engulfed me like a white shroud. As I struggled into them, the procession began. I waddled out, feeling like a penguin on land, the long candle in my hand swaying. Father Fred shot another of his patented looks, his lips pursed.

"That's a fire hazard, Chris!" his voice was an intense whisper.

He quickly had me swap the candle for the silver cross, sighed, and handed it to me.

Remembering the envelope my conscience and I fought silently over the rest of the mass. During the elevation of the Host, I was supposed to ring the chimes, a duty I relished. Still, the envelope's contents occupied my thoughts. Jon gave me a sly grin; his conscience was clear.

I rang those chimes, but my mind was elsewhere. I had extended them long enough for Father Fred to signal with a chopping motion, which I missed. I was too distracted to even enjoy my time on chime duty. I was troubled, so I had to act.

I explored the envelope's interior with my eyes. My eyes spotted the unmistakable shade of dark green that I have only ever seen on American currency. The sight of the money still surprised and horrified me.

Quietly, the church fell silent. Heat crawled up my neck. Behind me, I heard Jon's muffled laughter. I was too busy gasping to laugh. I closed the envelope and jammed it back into my front pocket. But not before I was able to see through the window envelope two $20 bills. It was my worst nightmare. It was something valuable. The weight of it was heavy on my mind. I was so laser-focused on the $35 needed to buy my own Montgomery Ward 10-speed bike that I quickly realized the envelope had enough money for it.

For a brief moment, I pictured myself joyfully shifting the gears of my new 10-speed. I even caught myself smiling. But that moment didn't last. Out of the corner of my eye, I swear the Virgin Mary statue was glaring at me scoldingly. But even worse than feeling the disappointment of the mother of Christ, I imagined the aging, trusting lady and the hurt in her heart if I had done anything other than place it in the collection plate. I respected her absolute faith in my brother and me to do the right thing. I had no choice; I had to return it.

After tucking the envelope deep into my pocket and feeling its corners against my thigh, I decided to do as she requested. I said a silent Hail Mary for Mrs. Gonzalez and another for myself. With the last song concluded and the final incense gone after mass, Jon and I helped Father Fred stack hymnals and move chairs. He winked at us, then guided us behind the altar to the narrow room where someone emptied the collection baskets into a battered safe.

Jon said, *"Moment of truth."* He elbowed my ribs, and not gently. Rubbing my ribcage, I placed the envelope with shaking hands in the basket designated for the offering envelopes. Mrs. Gonzalez's name in a looping blue script perched above a row of twenties. I always respected Jon for never questioning me and my integrity; he knew I would not keep the money. He still had to act as the responsible elder sibling, prompting me toward proper action.

God tested me, and I succeeded. Jon and I stepped out of the church, the heavy wooden doors creaking shut behind us. The air outside felt cooler, the chaotic noise of the world rushing back in to fill the void left by the church's serenity. Jon clapped me on the back with a bit too much force, his grin wide and triumphant. *"Well, well, little bro, looks like you're not such a lost cause after all."* I rolled my eyes at him, but a small smile tugged at the corners of my lips. For me, this moment was a turning point. It allowed me to prove something to myself, as well as to Mrs. Gonzalez and Father Fred.

Relief, mixed with a strange sense of pride, was what I felt as I mounted my old Schwinn bike to return home, the memory of the envelope still pressing against my thigh. As the wind whipped through my hair, carrying with it the smell of cut grass and distant laughter, I pedaled alongside Jon; the midday sun baked us. I am 100% confident that Jon slowed down his Raleigh 10-speed bike so I could keep pace with him, acknowledging his pride in his little brother for winning the internal battle against temptation. The memory of the envelope held a secret that could have altered everything, now serving as a tangible reminder of my choice to uphold integrity in the face of temptation. *...But I couldn't help but think..."* Man, that 1 speed would still be nice to have."

***

When finishing retelling that life lesson in morality, Chris said to Mara. "I still look back at that story with pride, and maybe I turned out pretty good as a result of that."

4

A Day In The Life

The more time our nostalgia hunters spent in the storage unit, the more worried Chris became. There was a problem Mara seemed to have lost track of; they needed to find that birth certificate. The climate for immigrants to the US could be unpredictable. The two of them needed to find the birth certificate to continue processing Mara's application for US citizenship. The clock was ticking. When dealing with governmental red tape, it's best not to tempt fate. Otherwise, it would not have been impossible for Mara to find herself sent back to Caracas. But now, she was too busy getting tangled in this nostalgia web herself.

"Oh my God!" Mara exclaimed, her laughter bubbling up like a stream that couldn't be held back. Her eyes sparkled with the kind of laughter that made you feel lighter just by being near her. She leaned back in her chair, shaking her head as if she couldn't believe what she was about to say. "It's always Catholic school or church... I swear, there's some kind of obsession with bodily functions!"

Her words hung in the air, laced with humor that hinted at shared experiences or ridiculous memories. I couldn't help but laugh along, though I wasn't entirely sure where she was going with this. As her laughter softened, she leaned forward again, her elbows resting on the table between us. She had this way of pulling you into her stories, as though you were living them with her.

"It reminds me," she began, her tone shifting slightly as her smile turned nostalgic. "There was this one time—oh, my God—I had to stay after school. The entire class did." She paused for effect, the corners of her mouth twitching as though trying to hold back another burst of laughter. "And do you know why? Because of a "moco!""

I blinked at her, trying to process what she'd just said. "Wait... what?" My eyebrows shot up in disbelief. "A moco"? Like... a booger?" My lips quirked into an incredulous grin as I tried to picture what on earth could have led an entire class to be punished over something so absurd.

"Yes! A "moco"! Can you believe it? Mara's laughter erupted again, her shoulders shaking as she briefly covered her mouth with one hand. She waved the other dismissively, as though brushing off the memory, though amusement still danced across her face.

"But wait," I pressed playfully, leaning closer now, caught up in the ridiculousness of it all. "You can't just drop something like that and not tell me the whole story."

Mara shook her head firmly, though her grin remained. "Nope," she said, dragging out the word teasingly. "That's a story for another day." She tilted her head mischievously, clearly enjoying leaving me hanging.

"You're cruel," I joked, sitting back with a mock pout. But just then, Mara found another old photo that brought the laughter to a halt. She showed the picture to me, and instinctively knew who was in the photo. She had heard a lot about the kid in the photo. "Yes, that isn't so easy to talk about... he was not just my friend, he was my best friend... and he should still be here." Knowing what I meant, Mara asked me, "Tell me more about him"......

***

10am –Happy Birthday

In the summer of 1978, I had a very predictable routine. Cereal for breakfast at the kitchen table while I studied the box scores from the previous day's major league baseball games. On a particular day in July, while eating my Cap'n Crunch, Life was good. Also on that day was my mother's birthday. Therefore, I diverted my typical summer routine a bit.

Once again, my best friend, Barnsy, hatched a plan to come over to my house to surprise my mother. Barnsy was the funniest, lighthearted, and kind person I had ever met. He knew well that my mother adored him, and she really, really did. She probably loved him the way everyone else did, and for the same reasons. I never saw him angry during his brief life. Never. He also usually had a smile on his face. Barnsy came from a big family, and he lived a quick bike ride away from me in the summer of 1978. We have been going to the same school since we were in kindergarten together. I can remember envying his SSP race car during the free play time we had inside our kindergarten classroom. The old SSPs ran by placing a long, plastic, T-shaped stick beside the wheels of the car. Barnsy had the name-brand racer; it could do jumps and other tricks. The one my parents bought me was an imitation, of course. But petty jealousy aside, Barnsy and I became instant friends.

***

Happy Birthday to you... Happy Birthday to you...

Mom was wiping down cabinet doors while I crunched the last soggy bits of cereal when we heard it—Barnsy's voice, off-key and earnest, floating up the creaky side stairs. He appeared in our kitchen doorway, red-faced and grinning, a folded construction paper card clutched in his hand. Mom's face lit up in a way I rarely saw in our household of grunt-talking males, who treated emotions like live grenades. She pressed the homemade card to her chest after reading it, something none of us would have thought to make her. Years later, at some cousin's wedding reception, I watched a tipsy Barnsy charm my mother into doing tequila shots, her laughing in a way that made her look young again. Barnsy, uniquely, managed this without behaving poorly. *Only Barnsy.*

11:30AM - Thank God For No Caller ID

After making my mother's day, Barnsy and I were off to do what 13-year-old boys do best: cause mischief. Gen X kids like Barnsy and I had a much longer leash. After wishing my mother a happy birthday, we rode our bikes to his house for a little unsupervised afternoon. Barnsy and I would routinely sleep over at each other's houses. All we had to do was call home and alert our parents of our plans. But both of us had baseball games later that evening. So, our mischief was limited to indoor hijinks to conserve our energy. As for mischief, we made prank phone calls. You could do that back then because no call tracing technology had been developed. Barnsy was the absolute master of prank calls. His calls were never malicious. His charm allowed him to keep the prankee engaged in a conversation longer than expected during phone calls. Other times, he would prey on unsuspecting businesses. At least at first, they were gullible. Barnsy loved to strike one business serially. Barnsy's facial expression changed suddenly.

A mischievous glint lit up Barnsy's eyes, a mischievous idea taking shape in his mind. Without a word, he reached for the rotary phone on the side table, his fingers dancing over the numbers. The familiar tone of Pizza and More's order taker filled the room, and Barnsy launched into his usual routine.

"Hello, this is Pizza and More. How can I help you?"

Barnsy: "Yeah, I'd like to order a large pizza....and some Smores,"

"Smores?"

Barnsy: "Yep, a large pizza and some S'mores, I'm hungry and I've looked forward to this all day. "

"We don't have S'mores, but pizza? I can give you that. "

Barnsy: "No S'mores?.... it won't be the same...man."

Barnsy must have called Pizza and More than 2 dozen times that summer. The same conversation about adding s'mores to the order repeated itself. I can remember one lazy summer afternoon when he called the doomed pizza shop. After he went into his never-ending request for the addition of stores to his order, the response from the annoyed soul on the other end of the line was thus:

"Smores???.... Why would you think we have Smores?"

Barnsy: "Well, the name of your place says it in the name! A pizza and SMORES."

"NO!!! GODAMMIT!!!Pizza and MORE...not a pizza and SMORES"

Barnsy: "Oh man... that changes things...I want nothing then. "

The commitment that Barnsy had to that gag was impressive. He waited months for someone to ask him why he wanted S'mores at a pizza joint. Brilliant.

Eventually, we grew tired of calling Pizza and More, so we retreated to "Barnsy's" bedroom, to his stereo and Beatles records.

1pm– Speaking words Of Wisdom

Barnsy flipped through his collection of records, his fingers tracing the worn *covers with a sense of reverence. It was one of the few things that could bring out a rare intensity in his otherwise carefree demeanor. That intensity was reserved for his comprehensive collection of Beatles music. Everything they ever recorded, he had in his collection.*

Before that summer, music had yet to make a dent in my consciousness the way baseball or books had. I still listened to the hits of the day on AM radio. But through Barnsy's influence, I now appreciated the sounds that came from the records on his turntable. His care of these records was meticulous. Every record had to be neatly placed back in the album's jacket cover, but not before he would go over it with a special cloth sponge before it passed inspection. No fingerprints, no lint, nothing. Only after the record passed inspection was it allowed back in its secure home. We did not take such precautions with the records at my house. That is why I couldn't help but notice how great Barnsy's records sounded compared to mine.

As the Beatles' melodies filled the room, Barnsy handpicked another record from his collection with a look of reverence on his face. He pulled out an album with a distinct blue color. Cross-referenced; it stood immediately next to a red-colored album that, aside from the color, could have been the blue album's twin brother. The red album's label shows the dates 1962–1966, but the blue one he chose had a label reading 1967–1970. His fingers moved delicately, almost reverently, over the worn cover, a sense of nostalgia and passion clear in his every movement. Watching him, I felt a newfound appreciation for music, one that had blossomed under Barnsy's influence.

The room seemed to shrink as the needle touched the vinyl, transporting the two friends into a world of melodies and lyrics. I remember hearing "Let it Be" and "Hey Jude" and a handful of other songs that I knew belonged to the Beatles. Songs that stood the test of time, songs that even now remain relevant, and I was just now getting to experience the songs that only true Beatles fans were familiar with. I felt special, like part of a secret society of music aficionados. Being just 13, I didn't know that this Beatles club was not exactly exclusive. They were the most popular band of all time. I felt important. The song that caught my attention that day was the song "I am The Walrus".

The room seemed to vibrate with energy, the air heavy with the weight of the music and the memories it carried. It was a moment frozen in time, a snapshot of two friends. As the last notes of the song faded into the air, the room fell into a brief silence, the echo of the music still reverberating in our minds. We exchanged a knowing look, this connection deepened by the shared experience of diving into the surreal world of the Beatles. We instinctively knew that this shared musical experience, this shared moment, would stay with us as long as we were friends. And then Barnsy farted, and the moment disappeared into a 13-year-old boy's audacity. Then laughter replaced the silence in the room.

"HAHAHAHA!!!!!!!"

4:30pm - Play Ball

Fast forward a few short hours, and Barnsy and I would be at the Boys and Girls Club baseball fields about 2 miles to the south of our neighborhood. The Boys and Girls' Club had 3 full-length, well-kept baseball fields. Teens and pre-teen baseball hopefuls, their parents, and a collection of fans of one sort or another packed the fields on Monday, Wednesday, and Thursday nights. Mostly other teenage friends of the players. One of those friends present was Eric Maldonado — more on him later.

Barnsy and I were on different teams, so we played on different fields. I went to my game, and Barnsy went to his. We would meet up after our games, stop at the 7-Eleven for post-game freezes, and then go back to his house, where we would sleep that night. That summer, we usually slept at each other's houses.

Pedaling into the 7-Eleven parking lot, we ran into Eric Maldonado, inexplicably nicknamed "Mick". Mick was a neighborhood kid whose father was a state police officer or FHP, Florida Highway Patrol. Mick went to public school, and he had a certain edge to him. Kind of a bad boy type, cops' kids usually are. Nonetheless, we also spent some time at his house when we were growing up. Mick's family had the only big yard in the neighborhood. It had great mango and oak trees that provided an ideal home base for our kick-the-can games. Mick was the shady character who would often hide in his house during kick the can. Inevitably, he would only come out of hiding for the call of:

"Olly Olly, all go free."

As he would of course shout, kicking the can and therefore winning that round. So, of course, it would come as no surprise that Mick would be the first kid my age to drink alcohol.

8:30pm - Just Say No

Barnsy and I were in front of the 7-Eleven, straddling our bike seats and slurping our freezes. Barnsy had a blue one, and mine was red. People have always said that if there was a food group I preferred, it would have been the "red food group". Those people were not wrong. Before we could even understand our freezees, Mick emerged without a bike from behind the 7-1Eleven. Barnsy and I were equally baffled to see Mick emerge from the back of the store. Both of us knew the only thing behind the 7-Eleven was bushes. Why did he appear from the shrubbery? What the hell was he doing back there? We didn't ponder that too long; we knew that was merely another example of Mick being Mick.

"Hey guys......what's up? What are you all doing?"

Mick didn't bother waiting around for answers to any of those questions. He was just there and invited himself on our trek home. The 3 of us worked our way back toward our houses. Mick on foot, me half walking and half riding my bike, and Barnsy riding his bike in circles around us as we made our way back to his house. Dusk was in full effect, and soon all the day's light would disappear to make way for another night. This had the feel of the type of nighttime that bad kids thirsted for.

We arrived at Mick's house first. Mick would bring another perspective to Barnsy and my sleepovers. The sleepovers at Barnsy's house were always fun. The atmosphere at his house was always much more relaxed. More kids and more kid energy and laughter. Barnsy's house was never at a loss for laughter, with his brothers and sister. They all had similar senses of humor and similar ways of interpreting our big blue marble. They also had HBO.

So, our plan that night was for the three of us to spend the night laughing and falling asleep in front of the TV, watching whatever movie or show was on. We didn't care about the show, but we knew it had a PG or an R rating, which made it forbidden *fruit for 13-year-old boys. So, we waited for Mick outside his house. He said he would be out soon because he just wanted to get his overnight stuff. So Barnsy and I waited, patiently at first. But more and more time elapsed as Barnsy and I sat on the ground, hoping to avoid the mangoes that were scattered across Mick's yard under the tree. Mick finally appeared. Surprisingly to no one, Mick exited his house through a door we weren't expecting. Exiting without any type of warning. Not even a "hey guys". He just did what he always does. He emerged, and the only way we knew he was approaching was by hearing a combination of footsteps and clanking. The clanking was coming from the duffel bag. Probably a military duffel bag that belonged to Mick's father. I hope the clanking wasn't another gruesome highway accident scene photo taken from the collection of work photos Mick's dad kept in a drawer in their kitchen. Why the kitchen? Don't know... don't want to know.*

Mick even lost track of where he was as he emerged from his house. Before he realized it, he was right on top of us, giggling. He had a strange, squeaky voice that he and his brothers all inherited from their mother. His mother, by the way, was a super sweet lady. But appearing over Mick's giggling was the unmistakable rattling of glass bottles. Me? I just brought a blanket and a toothbrush.

Mick: "Hey guys... let's stay here for a little while; my parents won't care. "

Me/Barnsy (simultaneously): "Sure, ok.... Whatever."

Before the echo of those words had even faded out, Mick revealed what was creating the clanking sound. It was a 6-pack of Rheingold Beer that Mick had stolen from his father's tightly guarded stash. Because it took Mick an eternity to appear from his house, I imagined it was indeed tightly guarded. I was in stunned silence. We were only 13 years old! This wasn't something I was ready for. I didn't think Barnsy was prepared for it either. I knew Mick was. Looking back, Barnsy was a good kid, very moral and honest. However, he was definitely braver and more adventurous than I was, and he didn't have the same fear of parents and consequences that I did.

PSSTpptt.... PssspTpp.... SSSSSSptt

The sound of Mick opening all three bottles with what I'm sure was probably some sort of fancy army bottle opener was music to my ears. But I'll never know for sure; it was pitch black under that mango tree. No doubt that this was the perfect setting for a clandestine operation. I'm sure Mick opened all three bottles himself — less about manners and more about laying down a challenge. In fact, despite the blackness of nighttime under the mango tree and in his backyard, I could feel him smiling as he handed Barnsy and me our bottles. I felt myself step back and pause, frozen. Thankfully, as I did this, both Mick and Barnsy took gulps of the forbidden nectar. I hesitated, but I wanted to do more than hesitate. I tried to retreat. Nancy Reagan's "just say no" wasn't a thing yet, but I wanted to say "no." I know it was just minutes, but it felt like hours, days... weeks. Saying no would make them see me as weak, a goody-goody. I looked at Barnsy. There were no signs of his inward struggle, no signs of his inner dialogue telling him it was wrong. He and Mick looked like they were kings of the jungle. Lions, men. Me? All I could see was my mother's image, crying. Haha... Saying to herself, "Where did we go wrong?" Geez, and that image appeared to me even without taking a sip of the beer." I couldn't imagine how strong it would be if I had, or if I came home drunk. Reputation, acceptance.... This was my first exposure to these teenage concepts, and it would not be my last...ohhh boy, for sure it would not be my last. The thought even occurred to me that if I were sleeping at Barnsy's house, my parents would never even find out. I could do it and get away with it!!!

Before that night, I did not know how strong the scent of beer could be. Maybe because it was Rheingold? Who knows.... If I said no, I risked being judged by my best friend. I even felt that if I said no, he could view it as a betrayal. But one thought kept popping into my 13-year-old mind. It was my mother's birthday, and this is not the way I expected it to finish............ But.... as Lennon/McCartney once wrote, that was A Day in the Life. But this was my life... For the record, I said no.

***

Mara smiled with tenderness as Chris finished that story. She was surprised by how much her husband revealed to her. He had always been very tight-lipped about his past in general and his childhood in particular. Mara's smile was different now: not that sly, ironic grin she reserved for the everyday absurdities of life in a new country, but a softer, more reverent expression, tinged with the faintest ache. It played on her lips as Chris's voice faded. He had just shared with her a story she had never heard, a slice of his young self.

5

Coño! Carajo! Mierda!

Sensing the tone in the storage unit needed lightening, Mara came across an old photo of her husband. Not as he is now. Not the bashful "Monaguillo" presenting the body and blood of Christ. But as a more confident-looking Chris saw the photo, his expression shifted, displaying both a grin and a chuckle. The photo revealed a young man wearing a baseball uniform. Mara traced her fingers over the faded image of her husband in that uniform, a hint of a smile tugging at the corners of her lips. The photograph captured a version of him she had never known, a young man filled with a confidence that seemed to radiate from the glossy paper. She raised her eyebrows in a gesture of approval as she held the photo for Chris to see.

Chris said. "Ahhhhh, that's me as a 16-year-old high school beisbolista".

A smile and a small laugh crossed Chris's face. "What's so funny?" Mara asked.

"Wait, keep looking in the box, that looks newer, and maybe the important documents are in that one. That birth certificate is here somewhere."

Even Chris became distracted from the task at hand. Studying the photo Mara was holding, he answered her question.

"Coach Horton... that is what is so funny," Mara, loving their trip down memory lane, said, "I love these photos..." Chris's countenance shifted into a grin, then a chuckle. Coach Horton was Chris's role model, and he always talked about how much he owed him. Dave Horton was a long-time teacher,

31

coach, and role model to hundreds of young men, but none other than Chris. Mara couldn't help but smile as she watched Chris reminisce about his younger self in the baseball uniform. The way his eyes lit up with a mixture of nostalgia and amusement made her heart swell with affection. She listened intently as he mentioned Coach Horton, a figure from his past who seemed to hold a special place in his memories.

As Chris spoke about the impact Coach Horton had on his life, Mara's admiration for her husband deepened. She could sense the genuine gratitude and respect in his voice, and it painted a vivid picture of the mentorship and guidance he had received during his formative years. Moments like these made Mara fall in love with Chris all over again, as she saw the layers of his character unfold before her.

Mara reached out and placed a hand on Chris's arm, a silent gesture of understanding and support. She knew these memories were precious to him, a glimpse into a past that had shaped the man he had become. "Every day, I see a little of Coach Horton in me. I'm the teacher I am today because of him.

"I feel another story coming on", said Mara. Chris laughed and said, "Oh yes......this is one of my favorites. I could tell 1000 Coach Horton stories, but right now this one is entering my mind................the year was 1997". This story is a lot more recent. But there are a few stories within this story because it's worth telling the stories of Dave Horton, the coach, and Dave Horton, the teacher. "Here comes another flashback," said Mara.

***

Mark Oliver let the screen door slam behind him, bringing the wet, heavy scent of the November storm into the house. He didn't bother to wipe his feet. He just stood there on the edge of the Persian rug, dripping onto the worn threads, a conquering general surveying the vanquished. Claude Perez and I, arranged on the sofa like nervous courtiers, stopped breathing. The only sound was the groan of the La-Z-Boy as Coach Dave Horton shifted his weight, the throne adjusting to its king.

For a long minute, no one spoke. The air in the living room was already thick with the ghosts of stale cigars and thirty years of Friday nights, but now it crackled with something new. Defeat. Humiliation. The final score hung between us, unspoken: Everglades 12, Palmer 10.

Oliver finally broke the silence. He unzipped his gleaming Everglades Prep rain jacket—a blue so offensively bright it seemed to mock the faded Palmer Pirates calendar on the wall—and let it fall over the back of an empty chair. He looked past me, past Claude Perez, his eyes locking on the man in the recliner.

"Eggelston should have scooped and scored," Oliver said. His voice was casual; an autopsy performed with a butter knife.

From the depths of the La-Z-Boy, Horton's reply was a low growl. "Thanks, Mark. Ya think?"

The sarcasm was thick enough to stand a spoon in. Horton didn't move, didn't even turn his head. He commanded the room from his recliner, just as he had commanded the sidelines and the classrooms. He was the sun; the rest of us were just chunks of rock caught in his orbit. Perez and I were loyal moons. Oliver was the rogue planet, the one who'd broken formation a year ago for a bigger paycheck and a waterfront field at Miami's most prestigious private school. A field where, as the local sports writers loved to say, an errant kick could splash down next to a sailboat.

Oliver just chuckled, a dry, grating sound. He sauntered over to the liquor cabinet, a sacred space no one entered without Horton's permission, and picked up the bottle of Jim Beam. "Dave, c'mon."

"Mark," Horton warned, his voice dropping another octave. "Don't mess with me right now."

I saw Perez flinch, ready to play peacekeeper, to launch into some bland analysis of the torrential rain or the slickness of the ball. I braced myself for the explosion. This was why these nights existed—to dissect the game, to assign blame, to re-forge the bonds of shared battle, win or lose. But Oliver winning and standing here in Horton's own living room was a violation of the natural order. It felt like sacrilege.

To my surprise, Oliver backed off. He put the bottle down and raised his hands in a gesture of mock surrender. Maybe he felt a pang of guilt for the win, for leaving his best friend of three decades to coach a scrappier team with less money and even less luck. He sank into the armchair opposite Perez, and the silence, heavier this time, returned.

As for me, I'm the only one in this room who isn't a football coach. Coach Horton got me my job teaching English and coaching baseball at Palmer Prep five years ago. It was a favor for a former player who'd spent the past few years chasing adulthood, and Horton offered it up like the mentor he was. My role in this fraternity was simple: I was the cameraman. From the press box, I filmed every game on a clunky Camcorder, my eye pressed to the viewfinder, a passive observer of other men's struggles. I was the historian. The archivist. I had tapes going back years, a library of Horton's triumphs and, lately, his frustrations.

Horton's jaw was a knot of muscle. His knuckles were white where he gripped the arms of his chair. The lines on his face, carved by decades of sun and stress, seemed to deepen before my eyes. He was staring at a spot on the wall, replaying the final, fatal moment of the game: Josh Eggelston, senior linebacker, with a clear path to the end zone as the opponent's fumbled ball sat on the wet grass like a gift from God. All he had to do was pick it up. Scoop and score. Instead, he'd played it safe. He'd fallen on it. Inexplicably. My breath, waiting for the dam to break. The tirade. The fury. Then, Horton spoke, his voice a strangled roar that was equal parts agony and disbelief.

"Josh... fucking... Eggelston!"

And the tension shattered. A collective exhale filled the room. A slow smirk spread across Horton's face, cracking the stony mask. It started as a tremor in his shoulders, then erupted into a deep, hearty laugh that shook his whole body. He laughed until tears welled in his eyes, a man laughing at the sheer, cosmic absurdity of his own misfortune. Perez started laughing, a high-pitched giggle of pure relief. Even Oliver cracked a smile, the tension draining from his shoulders.

The king was still the king. He had absorbed the loss, processed the absurdity, and turned it into a joke on himself. He was in control again.

With the air cleared, the ritual could begin. Horton's laughter subsided, but the smile stayed. He swiveled his head toward me, his eyes twinkling with bourbon-fueled mischief. He picked up the massive, 32-ounce insulated travel mug from the end table beside him and, with a theatrical flourish, slammed it down. The metallic clang echoed in the room.

"BOY!" he bellowed, the old nickname hitting me with its usual mix of affection and humiliation.

I stood up. "Yes, Coach."

"You know the drill." He slid the mug across the table.

This was my other job. Designated driver, designated bartender. I took the mug and went into the kitchen, where the familiar geography of the Horton house felt like a second home. Ice to the brim from the noisy icemaker. A pour of Jim Beam that was more than generous—a four-count, maybe five. Top it off with a splash of ginger ale. I stirred it with a long spoon and brought the chalice back to him. He took a deep swig, his eyes closing in satisfaction. "Attaboy."

He gestured with his head to the others. "Alright. Let's not talk about that goddamn game anymore tonight. It's in the books. It's over." He took another drink.

Just then, Claude Perez blurted out to the room. "BOBO- kick it out of bounds!!" Perez's out-of-left-field statement brought a sizeable roar of laughter to the scene.

Sensing it was time to deflect from the king, Claude Perez decided to take one for the team. When he blurted that out, the room erupted with laughter. Everyone present knew exactly what "Bobo, kick it out of bounds" meant. Horton, through his laughter when recalling that story, said,

"Bobo, you could mess up a one-car funeral."

Claude Perez, who had been a hot-shot quarterback under Horton and was now his most loyal assistant, was safe now; on the solid ground of a story he'd heard and told a hundred times. A tale that reaffirmed the natural order of things.

"Okay, Coach, okay," he began, leaning forward, his voice taking on the cadence of a practiced storyteller. "So, it's my junior year, we're playing Northwest Christian. They're running us off the field. It's like 28-0 in the second quarter. They've already run back a punt and a kickoff. Our offense can't get a single first down." Perez would say.

I settled back into my armchair, content to be the audience. I knew this story by heart. I'd filmed the game, which came from.

"So, we're punting again," Perez continued, his hands painting the scene in the air. "I'm back there, the punter. They called me 'Bobo' back then, right? Because Coach says I got a head full of rocks."

Horton grunted in affirmation. "Still do."

"And Coach realizes," Perez said, pointing a thumb at Horton, "that there's no guarantee I'm going to do the smart thing. So he starts screaming from the sideline. From the press box, Chris, you could hear him, right?"

"Clear as a bell," I said.

"He's screaming, 'BOBO! BOBO! KICK IT OUT OF BOUNDS!' Perez's voice rose to an imitation of Horton's gravelly roar. "He wants me to angle it, right? Kick it away from their returner, who runs like a cheetah. A sound strategy."

Oliver was smiling now, a genuine smile. This was the Horton he loved, the one from the good old days.

"But I'm a good fifty yards away," Perez said, his eyes wide with feigned innocence. "Pads, helmet, the crowd... I can barely hear him. I just saw him waving his arm toward the sideline. I shrug, like, 'Okay, Coach, you got it.' The ball is snapped, it's perfect. I catch it, take my steps..." He paused for dramatic effect.

"And then," he said, his voice dropping to a conspiratorial whisper, "I shrug again, pivot ninety degrees, and punt the ball directly over Coach's head, straight into our own bench. A net loss of, what, seventeen yards?"

The room erupted in the laughter I knew was coming.

"I watch the ball sail over his head," Perez howled, wiping a tear from his eye. "And the whole stadium goes quiet for a second. And then, over the silence, you just hear Coach Horton's voice, not even yelling, just... full of wonder. He just says, 'What... the... fuck?'"

Horton was shaking with laughter, slapping the arm of his La-Z-Boy, and he said, "You even squared up directly to our sideline."

"And then he does it," Perez finished, the punchline landing perfectly. "He finds me on the sideline, his hand goes to his hat, and he turns the bill sideways on his head. The hat turn. The universal sign for, 'You are the dumbest son of a bitch I have ever had the misfortune to coach.'"

The story landed, a perfect, comforting balm on the raw wound of the night. It was a story about a loss, but a meaningless one from long ago, burnished by time into a funny anecdote. It was a story where Horton was in complete control, the wise, witty, cantankerous godhead of our little universe. He took a long pull from his mug, finishing nearly half of it. He looked over at Oliver, a challenge in his eyes.

Finally, Horton turned to me and said, "OK Hemingway, spin your tale... what's your war story tonight?" I smiled and simply said, "My essay exam." Horton smirked and said. "You thought you were so damn smart, didn't you?"

"Ladies and gentlemen, welcome to the Dave Horton roast.", Mark Oliver quipped.

Sensing this was my moment to shine, I wanted to weave a detailed web in my Horton war story. He is a complex man with many layers, some of which are hidden. So with precision, I told a story of Dave Horton, the teacher, not just in the classroom, but also as a presence throughout the entire school building. How did he even command the hallways?

As Coach Horton would stroll to his classroom, he would say hello to every kid, first bump others, and even "Vulcaned" one unsuspecting freshman. The Coach Horton "Vulcan" was a pinch on the shoulder designed to inflict playful pain. Playful as it was, it still hurt. The next bell rang, and Coach Horton took his place at the teacher's desk at the front of the room. Over his left shoulder, covering the chalkboard was a vast, pull-down map of the State of Florida. He stayed in his seat and rolled his teacher chair in range of the map, and he yanked the bottom of it, and it violently snapped and rolled its way back from where it came. When the map flew up, it concealed the questions for a Unit Test in world history.

"COMPARE AND CONTRAST THE EFFECTS OF THE INDUSTRIAL REVOLUTION ON THE CITIES IN THE NORTH VS. THE AGRICULTURAL ECONOMY OF THE SOUTH?"

Coach Horton loved essay exams for his History Classes. Educationally, he was ahead of his time. Being an English teacher too, he understood the value of writing as a cross-curricular tool. Or was it because essay exams were easier to create? My opinion is that the answer is a little from "A" and a little from column "B". I sat in my traditional back row seat, doing my best to attract as little attention as possible. I just put my head down and attacked that essay exam. I also loved essay exams. I *always figured that if the style you write the essay in and the amount of time you took to construct a well-written essay, the less you had to depend on the actual correct answer. So this played to my strength. So, in the comfort of my Senior year, I decided to get a bit creative and have some fun with this exam.*

Within the context of the essay, sandwiched in between 'Many factories in the northern cities required a lot of manpower' and 'thus began the great migration', and slyly placed in the middle of a paragraph, I wrote the following.

"Coach Horton, I don't believe you actually read the entirety of everyone's essays. I believe you assign a grade based solely on reputation."

And without missing a beat, I continued with the essay.

With a deep breath, I set my pen down and leaned back in my chair, trying to appear nonchalant as I awaited the inevitable. Would Coach Horton catch his daring statement, or would it slip through unnoticed like a whisper in the night? I truly believed in my statement. In my days as his student, I never really recognized how brilliant a teacher he was. I always thought he considered himself too cool and too experienced to subscribe to anything new. Because of this, I mislabeled him as lazy, thinking he would never see my comment and give me my "A". Haha. I was wrong. Without ever saying a word, only giving me his trademark smile/smirk where no teeth are present, he simply wrote in the margin the following:

"You are wrong, Chris, I read every word of every essay" ....

"Chris, I think you were right. There is no way he read all those essays," said Coach Oliver as everyone laughed in agreement.

"Smooth!! I am smooth", Horton said as he remembered that story. However, no night at Casa de Horton would ever be complete without seeing the real head of the household, Coach's wife, Maria. Maria entered the room with her trademark grace. When she entered the room, the four of us sat up a little straighter, as if we were all transported back to school and the principal unexpectedly entered the room. Actually, the principal had arrived— the current principal at St. Mary's Academy, an all-girls Catholic school. Maria kept the coach in check; even he straightened up when she entered the room. He knew that he was the second-best teacher in his house. The first family of education was a newly formed romantic couple when I first met them, and Maria was my ninth-grade math teacher at Jesuit.

Maria's entrance into the room was a subtle hint to Dave that the night needed to start wrapping up. Catching her husband's eye with that look wives perfect over decades of marriage—the silent signal that four tipsy teachers were getting rowdy enough for the neighbors to notice. As Maria was exiting the room, she bid goodnight to the boys. She reminded Dave that the back bathroom would be unavailable because she was about to begin her pre-sleep routine. Before she disappeared down the hallway, she called back to him.

Maria:" Hun...don't forget to let 'Lady' out before you come to bed"

"Lady" was Horton's Golden Retriever and the sweetest dog ever. He raised a hearty 'thumbs up' gesture in her direction, reaching behind him to open the sliding glass door that led to the back yard. "Lady" happily bounded out into the night. The 4 of us picked up the subliminal message from Maria to her husband, even if he didn't. We all commented jokingly to Horton how great she was, and to borrow a football cliche, how he had "outkicked his coverage". Our laughter started to simmer down, and the volume of the room did too. With the screen door open to the backyard, soothing nighttime sounds were now audible. Finally, an unexpected noise from the outside appeared: it increased in volume and recognizability.SPLAS HHHHH....SPLUNKKKK........SPPPLASSSHHHH! It was rhythmic. For the first time all night, there was a brief silence. The silence lasted long enough for everyone to shout with laughter.....IT'S LADY!!!! SHES IN THE POOL!!!! We all got up, and Claude Perez threw back the back curtain to confirm. From there, we could see Lady having the time of her 12-year-old life, doing what Golden Retrievers do — swim.

Horton: "Cono!!!!Carajo!!!Mierda!!!!"

Realizing he forgot to close the pool gate, Horton rushed outside, as much as someone with five bourbons in his stomach was able to. Arriving at the pool, he was able to eventually convince Lady to exit the pool. He didn't even have to dive in himself!!! That was the good news..........what happened next was the event that made this evening much more entertaining than even the funniest war story could ever produce.

Hearing the raised voice of her master's impending crash out, Lady knew she was in trouble. She hurried back into the house. Through the open sliding glass door, through the living room, and finally, down the hall leading to the master bedroom.

Uh oh....

To add insult to injury, in addition to leaving the pool gate door open, Dave doubled down on his mistake. He also left the bedroom door open. Yep.......Lady, of course, accepted the invitation to jump on the king-size bed where Dave and Maria rest their weary heads to sleep. Once on top of the bed, "Lady," now with all the lush blond fur that makes a golden retriever golden, proceeded to shake. Shake with all her fury (and furry), not once, not twice, but easily a dozen shakes. Droplets of water, fur, slobber, did I mention fur? It all made its way onto the bed; the blankets, sheets,pillows, and even the headboard were damp.

Perez, Oliver, and I didn't stick around for the aftermath. But we did clean up the living room of any mess we made. We needed something to do while Coach Horton was sequestered in a closed-door meeting as soon as Maria got out of the shower. As we walked outside, someone said, "Wow, what a night...someone could write a book about it." I chuckled and said, "You're right, someone could" .....Coño Carajo Mierda Indeed.

***

6

Gabriel's Horn

Looking to solve the problem at hand, Chris attempts to reassure Mara about the birth certificate that has not yet been found. He offered this solution for Mara to ponder.

"OK, Mara, time is not our friend now. From here to downtown it'll be about a 20-minute drive. If we are going to the courthouse, we need to leave here by 4 pm." Mara thought about that and asked, "What time is it now? 3:30? OK, let's look for a few more minutes."

As she said, she discovered something in yet another box. Mara held up a monaguillo's complete and remarkably well-preserved cassock and gown. A puzzled Chris looked at it and said, "Where did that come from....I don't recognize it." Mara said to him. "How can you not recognize this? We've already seen 100 photos of you in the "Monaguillo" uniform. "True, but look, that cassock is red.......all of the others are black.....we only wore red on special masses, like Christmas midnight mass....you know, "noche buena." Mara didn't understand his puzzlement. Finally, Chris said, "The priests did not let us anywhere near any of the big masses."

"Why??" Mara asked. To that, Chris replied, "WELLLL........there was one time when........ "

"Is it time for another flashback?" Mara asked. Chris answered, "It sure is."

*****

My brother Jon and I took our places at the kitchen table. We had all of our family meals at this table, and where Jon and I consume our breakfasts before departing for church. The church in question is called "Church of the Garden". Our neighborhood church and the church where we served as "monaguillos" or altar boys. Jon is 6 years my senior. Our eldest brother Frank is upstairs sleeping. I'm not sure when Frank stopped being an altar boy, but he did well in avoiding Jon and me on the altar. Jon, the prototype of a middle child, was mischievous, mercurial, and the family clown and charmer, but he had a heart that outmatched both Frank and me in kindness. Frank was the oldest and most accomplished of us. Even today, I recall that he, as a youth, possessed more maturity than Jon and me. However, even asleep, he could never get 100% rest. I can recall that during this period, we got a Dachshund puppy named "Fraulein". Jon and I, in our constant search for laughter, would use "Fraulein" as a tool for mass disruption against Frank. We would throw her dog toys on Frank's bed or even the couch where he liked to nap, tantalizing the energetic weiner dog puppy to jump on Frank, fetch her toy, and disturb his nap.

ASince I was the youngest, my bond with my brothers was quite different from the relationships my friends had with their closer siblings of a similar age. My relationship with my brothers comprised envy, antagonism, and distance, with some idol worship sprinkled in. I was envious that they had each other; I had always dreamed of having a sibling my age. And like all siblings, we fought, fought a lot. These fights were always 2 on 1. The odd one out changed every time. Maybe it was Frank and me versus Jon, or Frank and Jon versus me. It was rotational. However, the aspect of my view of my older brothers that stood out the most was idol worship. I welcomed opportunities to interact with them outside; they were my idols.

But I digress; this story is one of pure mischief. It is about the day that Jon and I, with help from my best friend, Barnsy, "Big John" aka John Barnett, nearly brought down the ecclesiastical hierarchy of the Church of the Garden, risking eternal damnation as defined by our mother. First, some context. Knowing that we can be a demanding group, my father requested that our mom deserve a day to sleep in. She consistently left us by ourselves on Sunday mornings, under firm direction: (1) avoid burning down the house, (2) allow Frank his sleep until noon, and (3) please, be presentable and punctual for altar boy duties. But being presentable was a heavy lift. Jon's idea of "church clothes" was the same ratty polo shirt he wore to school, now decorated with a Rorschach splotch of syrup. A wet palm flattened my hair, only stressing the contours of my cowlick, giving me a windswept look even in the kitchen. We didn't fit the nuns' preference at Our Lady of Perpetual Discipline because we weren't polished, solemn children. We departed through that entrance, onto our bicycles, and then cycled toward the church.

At that instant, we halted our bikes beside the church, then Barnsy appeared from the fence. His yard and house were behind the church. We did everything together. Played baseball, listened to his Beatles records, and even made prank phone calls together. He was my best friend and my partner in crime. Jim, his older brother by three years, was also there. The four of us together climbed the stairs behind the church, which led to the sacristy, where mass preparations unfolded. In the sacristy were the sacramental wine, the body of Christ, hosts, crosses, candles, and various other items. So the four of us prepared for the 9 a.m. Sunday mass. There was nothing holy about the sacristy on a Sunday morning. It smelled of floor polish, stale incense, and the vague, medicinal tang of cheap Communion wine. The four of us took our roles with varying degrees of solemnity. Jim, who was the leader for this mass, set about lining up the cruets and polishing the chalice. Jon rummaged through the drawers and cabinets under the pretense of "inventory inspection." Still, he was looking for matches and altar candles to melt and reshape into crude little sculptures. Barnsy and I busied ourselves by stealing glances through the peephole that looked onto the audience, providing live commentary on the early arrivals. "And here comes Jumpin' Jim Bennett....yes, folks, it appears he is wearing the same pants for the 4th day in a row", said Barnsy in his best play-by-play announcer voice.

"Alright, it's time", Father Fred said as both he and the faint scent of cigarettes entered the sacristy. Father Fred was our parish's cool priest. The altar boys respected him, even with his gruff demeanor.   Truth felt present within the atmosphere. He coached the Parrish basketball team, which made him kind of cool. Some priests try to act hip or cool to relate to the young parishioners. Still, their efforts seem forced, making them appear lame and inauthentic. Father Fred didn't need to force anything. One could discern that he did not have a typical priestly experience before entering the order. I don't think he ever spent time in cloisters of any kind. We felt at ease with him, which made us less anxious than we were around their priests. So when the scent of his cigarettes entered the room, we hopped to attention and prepared ourselves for the main event, or in this case, the 9am Sunday mass.

It was a typical Sunday 9 a.m. mass. Those individuals, by force of habit, attended the gatherings. The "Church of the Garden's" weekend mass schedule was Saturday at 3 p.m. and 5:30 p.m. The Saturday 5:30 and Sunday noon masses were the two most highly attended masses. That was when the "A-team" worked. We were relegated to Sunday at 9 a.m.; we were not the "A" team. Because it was only the 9 a.m. mass, there was less Catholic pomp and circumstance. No procession originated behind the church towards the altar. The priest sprinkled no holy water. It was just a quick trip from the sacristy straight to the altar. Just Fr. Fred led the way with the Bible and Jim with the cross. John and Jon slinked behind me.

At this mass, you could see each bead of moisture on the stained glass windows, the kind where eyes drifted; the tired congregants in the front row blinked into the sunrise filtering through, and every kid in the pews was already checking the time. At least two parishioners in every row were hungover, judging by their slumping foreheads and the funereal pace at which they made the sign of the cross. The 9am mass couldn't justify the need for a full choir. Only Mrs Fox, the grammar school music teacher, was at the piano in the choir loft, and a straight-laced sixty-something in a pastel blouse warbled through "Peace is Flowing Like a River." For a second I thought time had doubled back on itself.

Brother Jon nudged me. "Check this," jerking his chin at the altar candles. I squinted. He'd stacked three of the candle ends and jammed a fourth into the top, creating a lopsided, waxen totem that flickered with every passing draft. Jon grinned with a proud glimmer of pride in his mischievous piece of art. Friend John and I were already on shaky ground, trying to hold back our laughter. This was a bad sign; we were not even 3 minutes into the mass.

Positioned on the sacred sanctity of the altar, Jon's candle totem wobbled there in *full view of God and everyone. While Father Fred recited the Gloria, Jon flicked at the makeshift tower with the back of his hand, making it quiver like an aspen. Beside him, Jim's nostrils flared in silent disapproval. Barnsy elbowed me so hard that I smacked my kneecaps on the marble step, which echoed like a cannon through the empty nave.*

I saw the ripple of movement out in the congregation—Mrs. De La Cruz, the holiest layperson known to man, stiffened in her pew. She must have caught the motion on the altar and now glared with the sort of nuclear intensity that could melt choir lofts. My mother called her "the Neighborhood Watch for the Lord." Mrs. De La Cruz now had a target for her venom. She studied every movement of ours now, and she reported it to my mom. This scared me to my core. It's why my dad sometimes referred to me as "Nervous Nelly". Jon, however, felt no such burden. I admired his fearlessness; he didn't fear the consequences of any kind. He slept like a baby at night; it would require a comprehensive count of every sheep in the entire country of Wales to get me to sleep.

The day's readings were heavy with the theme of "Vengeance is Mine."

When Father Fred motioned for the Offertory, I braced myself for disaster. Barnsy and I ferried the glass containers of water and wine from the table to the altar, a job requiring all the dexterity and hand-eye coordination of a lunar landing so no spills would occur. As I was halfway, I could hear Brother Jon making the sound "ooooh oooooo aaaahhhh", taunting me not to drop the blood of Christ. BBy the grace of St. Francis's image staring at me from his perch on the stained glass window behind the altar, I was able to deliver the chalice to its destination.

The Offertory continued, and I couldn't shake the feeling that disaster was looming over us like a dark cloud. Jon's mischievous glances only added to my mounting anxiety. I could hear Mrs. De La Cruz's disapproving whispers in my ear as we navigated the delicate task of presenting the gifts.

I went back to my assigned seat at the rear of the altar after I had made the gifts holy. Little did I know, the main mischief hadn't begun yet.

The statue of Saint Luke had its left eye chipped off, which always made it seem like he was winking at me, daring me to do something bad in the middle of Mass.

That Sunday, we were on our best behavior for the first fifteen seconds—record time if you asked my mom. Jon and I squeezed in next to Fr. Fred in our altar server robes, hands folded at chest height and faces blank with forced piety. Barnsy across the aisle with the incense boat grinned at me every time Fr. Fred turned his back. This seating arrangement was dangerous. Even in an environment where laughing was socially acceptable, once one of us laughed, the other would follow. However, this was not one of those socially acceptable times, and both Barnsy and I sensed we knew it could be a struggle today to refrain from laughter...... We weren't wrong.

I tried to focus on the ceiling. My nose buzzed with the resinous discharge from the candles Jon desecrated. Jon was eerily quiet, I noticed. That made me suspicious.

The cushions on the altar pews were thin, but they still provided a reasonable amount of comfort. However, they couldn't deaden vibrations within the pews. Brother Jon's comedic timing was unrivaled, and he was resourceful in using whatever was in his environment. He could sense the best moment to deliver his comedic boom. A spoken joke wasn't necessary; he could use a facial expression or pantomimed motion with his hands or even a particular type of body language. He cared little about his method of delivering jokes. This being the case, he waited for the perfect combination of silence. It seems he had a plan. Uh oh.....beware. But this wasn't the typical type of silence. This was a holy silence only experienced within a church. However, this quiet made up merely a part of the whole. He needed eye contact. Not just any eye contact; he waited for eye contact between Barnsy and me.

That moment arrived.

Fr. Fred presented himself and took communion, biting down on the host that represented the body of Christ. During quiet reflection, his solemn reflection. No one wished to disrupt that. Within the Roman Catholic mass, this moment is one of its most significant, with the entire congregation conscious of what it stands for. Everyone realized this moment requires absolute silence. Everyone but Jon, of course.

Just before we stood up. Jon made solid eye contact with me, paused, and then unleashed a fart reminiscent of Gabriel's horn. The pew beneath us vibrated like an earthquake, and the sound echoed throughout the altar with its impressive acoustics. It was loud—louder than Jon had intended. For a brief second, embarrassment flickered across his face, but it disappeared because of its unfamiliarity. Jon felt no *shame. Instead, he grinned with pride at his accomplishment.*

Barnsy and I were in stunned silence. We tried to hold back laughter. For almost 2 entire seconds, we were successful. However, the dam yielded, generating odd, constricted snorts. Barnsy gave in first. I could hold my laughter longer until, at the church's perimeter, somebody's grandma somehow interpreted the noise as sneezing, responding compassionately with, "Bless you." That was it for me. I burst under the pressure of trying to withhold my laughter.

Fr. Fred, never too far away from showing his "Irish temper", was seeing red.

He turned, the front of his vestments ballooning out a little with his movement, and gave the three of us the look. The look was so forceful that I swear the baby Jesus in the nativity scene winced in solidarity. His gaze, focused like a laser beam with nuclear-grade disappointment, froze us. Jon's feet shuffled. I willed my face into Stonehenge.

There's a chemical chain reaction to laughter. It doesn't dissipate like fog; it hangs around, ready to spark up again at the slightest provocation. Every tick of the clock, every hawk of a parishioner's throat, every accidental clang of silverware started the cycle anew, and each time, Fr. Fred's face got a shade more crimson.

The rest of Mass was an endurance event. Five more minutes of standing, kneeling, standing, memorizing, and trying to forget the sound of Fr. Fred's voice to the 3 of us, "WHAT IS WRONG WITH YOU??!!!" The worst part was that he didn't know it was Jon! So the 3 of us had to share the blame and his wrath.

I knew the consequences were fast approaching, and the best-case scenario, I figured, was a temporary exile from serving duties and a reeducation session in the church basement with Sister Mary Cecilia. Reporting to our parents presents the most undesirable situation, resulting in punishment that is more imaginative and permanent than anything Fr. Fred could dream up.

The Mass ended. That final hymn expressed triumph unlike any other. We scurried to the sacristy at a pace somewhere between Olympic sprinter and fugitive, colliding with Sister Mary Cecilia herself—who, to our shock, was suppressing a twitch of a smile beneath her formidable upper lip. She gestured toward the folding table holding clean linens. Jon started in on the linens, whistling "On Eagle's Wings" through his teeth, and Barnsy took to stacking hymnals with the quiet satisfaction of a man who knew he'd witnessed history. I was waiting for the proverbial other shoe to drop. Fr. Fred's shoe, I was worried it was going to fall and go through my gluteus maximus. I shot a worried look at brother Jon. "Don't worry, Nervous Nelly."

Fr. Fred closed the door with a thud that jolted loose a cluster of dust motes, and then stood there, hands steepled. He did not speak immediately. He just stared at us, letting the quiet pool in the small space until it felt like we might actually drown in it.

"Explain to me," his voice pitched low and precise.

Fr. Fred closed the door with a thud that jolted loose a cluster of dust motes, and then stood there, hands steepled. He did not speak immediately. He just stared at us, letting the quiet pool in the small space until it felt like we might actually drown in it.

"Explain to me," his voice pitched low and precise.

He let the words hang. I glanced at Jon, whose face had defaulted to its most innocent setting—mouth open, eyebrows up, the look of a kid who'd never once in his life contemplated farting, let alone weaponized it. Barnsy's complexion had gone the alarming color of communion wine.

"Which of you," Fr. Fred asked, "thought it would be...appropriate...to trumpet your—" here he paused, searching for the sacred language "—digestive lamentations during the consecration?"

No one answered. Somewhere in the sacristy, the ancient boiler rattled awake, its cough a kind of punctuation.

"Was it a joke?" Fr. Fred pressed. "A test of discipline? Or have I failed at conveying the seriousness of the mystery that you think of the Eucharist as an occasion for barnyard humor?"

Jon's cheeks puffed out. He was dying to answer. Jon's forthcoming words caused trepidation. He appeared ready to speak. He said, "It was me, Father. I'm sorry." I breathed a sigh of relief. I was worried he was going to add insult to injury by saying something outrageous. Thank God he showed restraint.

He even kept his face straight while he said it, which was how I knew Jon felt bad, or at least as bad as Jon ever could. There was a long pause. Fr. Fred's eyes narrowed, as if he were searching Jon for any sign of sarcasm or insolence, but for once, none was on offer.

I braced for the thunder, but Fr. Fred just exhaled, looking tired — the tired that only kids like us could inflict on a person. "Proceed," he offered, motioning toward the laundry basket. "You can finish the linens and then help Mrs. Palmer set up for the pancake breakfast. I'll think of something more...edifying for you next week." His voice softened. "You're good boys, but goodness is no excuse for stupidity. Understood?

*** *

7

The Cry Room

From within the steamy storage unit, Mara looked at Chris incredulously. She was still thinking about the last story.

"It's not too late to go to the courthouse now," Chris pointed out. "Mara said, 'I prefer to look in here.' If we try to get a new birth certificate, it may take more time, and we are only here for a few days." Chris was hoping to be free of this storage place and would say anything to leave.

"Boys will be boys, I guess", Mara said, not skipping a beat or acknowledging Chris's desire to leave. She was still knee deep in joy, hearing these stories about her husband. Even if the stories highlighted bodily functions. Once the incredulous look disappeared from her face, she couldn't help but feel some sadness for him. She was beginning to see the impact Barnsy had on Chris.

"You had a great friend, it sounds like you guys had so much fun together." After saying this, she stopped and went on to say, "I'm sorry... you miss him, don't you?"

"Oh my god, I just remembered the 'Cry Room'," Chris bellowed excitedly. He was already laughing, maybe more to deflect away from a potential sad moment. "Cry Room?" Mara asked. "What is the 'Cry Room'?" Chris looked at his watch: 3:58 p.m. "Okay, I'll tell the 'Cry Room' story super quick."

Mara bubbled with joy, "Flashback time!"

Well, in the back of our church we had...............

50

***

The week after the "Gabriel's Horn" incident, "Barnsy," my brother Jon, and I were told we had to serve a one-week suspension from altar boy duty. The 3 "Monaguillos" were on probation. We could not serve mass. No carrying the cross, no chime ringing, no laughing on the altar. When Sunday came, unsure of our purpose, the three of us attended mass anyway, out of habit. This time, we didn't have to ride our bikes. We got a ride. Don't assume this was a favor or something good. Our ride was dear old dad. Not good. For many reasons, it wasn't good, the most significant being his mandatory mass attendance. This also meant he suffered consequences.

Because my mother was working and could not attend this mass, it meant my father had to. As shown by the previous week's performance at mass, Mom wasn't keen on trusting Jon and me. So dad came with us, but at least we got a ride. To add to the bouillabaisse of the 9AM Sunday mass, my brother Frank had to attend mass. This was a direct order from dear old dad, under the heading of If I have to go? That means you also have to go. So I don't have to tell you how pleased both dad and Frank were that fine morning.

So off we went to church. Upon arrival, waiting for us near one of the side entrances was Barnsy. To that, my brother Frank chimed in by saying "There is the third", alluding to the third member of our suspension party. Barnsy laughed his mischievous laugh at Frank's comment. The five of us followed a single file behind my father, like ducklings behind the adult. We shuffled into the church and started making our way towards the back row of pews. But on our way, Barnsy motioned his head towards a door in the back of the church on the right as you entered. It's not a secret door; it's in plain sight. It is a door that leads to the most intriguing room of the entire church. TThe "Cry Room", whether that was even the official name for it. That is what everyone referred to it as. The room was rumored to be soundproof, and its function was to provide a quiet room for young parents to bring their babies if they started crying. My brother Jon and I were always fascinated by this room. We wondered whether it was soundproof.

We always wanted to test the validity of that claim. Our curiosity about the "Cry Room" was a frequent topic of conversation whenever we were in that church.

Barnsy went along on this ride with us. It was always he who suggested we test the soundproof claim. "Barnsy's" body language said, "Today is the day." Jon told Dad that the three of us were going to be in the "Cry Room" for the mass. Something had to entertain us due to our banishment from our usual "Monaguillo" duties. My father barely even acknowledged Jon as he told Dad our plan, but he approved of it.

The three of us settled into the "Cry Room" as all the other mass attendees settled into theirs. All the regular players were in place: Ms. De La Cruz, aka "Neighborhood watch for the Lord", Mrs. Fox, the choir lady, and everyone else who knew of our suspension from that day's mass. It wasn't our intention to be in the "Cry Room" in shame. But I have to admit it was a nice way to avoid the judging stares from Ms. De La Cruz.

The room was bigger than I initially thought. The room has two regular full-length church pews, a diaper changing table, and even speakers to hear the mass. Discovering all the various items inside the "Cry Room" occupied our attention until we heard the door open. We were surprised, and we weren't sure who was coming in. We should have predicted it was Fr. Fred. He entered the room and looked around as if to ensure the soundproofing could hold us, or at least silence Jon. After all, it was he who got us into this predicament. He then said.

"It seems we should have put the three of you in this room last week." The three of us kind of chuckled as he exited the "Cry Room" after having made that jab. It was funny. A few seconds later, the mass officially began. Jim Barnett was leading the way, carrying the cross. At the same time, a few other Monaguillos followed behind as they traversed the altar, eventually finding the seats on the altar that should have had us on them. Guilt and embarrassment set in as I watched the mass happen without me. The same regret did not burden the two Jo(h)ns I felt. Our focus quickly turned towards our original quest. Test to see if the room was as advertised. If it were soundproof.

It all started simply enough. First, it was just some hoots or hollers to test it. The three of us alternated "hooting", waiting to see if there was any response from the people in the first few rows.

"Hoot" ...HOOOOOt....... Woot....WWOOT"

Each added round of "hoots and woots" became increasingly louder. Every once in a while, we would stop to survey the congregation to see if anyone was looking in our direction. When that didn't happen, we continued. Not even Ms. De La Cruz seemed to hear us, and if she did, she wasn't turning around to glare at us disapprovingly.

"HOOOOOOOOTTTTTT"

The three of us harmonized, testing the boundaries of the "Cry Room". So far, so good. Maybe the room was soundproof. That's when things started to get interesting. The hoots and woo-woots turned into yells, then consistent yelling, and finally evolved into screams. Not sure if it was the sound or the fact that he instinctively knew we were up to no good, my brother Frank turned around a few times. It's gold to hear him retell it.

"So I turn around to see what you guys are doing, because I knew it couldn't be good. I was surprised to find how funny the imagery looked... Still frustrated, I even had to go to church that day. I expected to be annoyed at you guys... but that was impossible. I turn around and I see all three of you idiots with faces beet red, mouths wide open, and eyes showing rage, then it hit me- you guys were screaming at the top of your lungs!!!!" Frank's face was scrunched up with his eyes hidden, he was laughing so hard retelling this story, his recollection was funnier than the actual witnessing of the three of you screaming at top volume inside a room designed to help mothers calm babies down, a room, lest we forget, is inside a Catholic church. Let's not forget that we were supposed to be on the altar then. Frank continued..."Dad, sensing he should not have allowed the three of you unsupervised inside the "Cry Room", sent me in to check on you. From the back row of pews where we could clearly see, I was predicting something pretty funny....But what I got, I wasn't ready for. I didn't think I would contribute to this".

I remember it like it was yesterday. The way every head in that church shot back to the back of the church. The sound was deafening. Frank did not warn us he was coming to check on us. Much to our surprise, to his surprise, and to the surprise of every person in the church that day. Sound came rushing out the door of the "Cry Room", yep, you guessed it. Frank opened the "Cry Room" door in mid scream - and the sound of three suspended, adolescent "Monaguillos" poured out into the front of the church, bounced off the sacristy, and caromed out into the main congregation. The sound of us screaming caused everyone sitting in the pews to gasp and let out their own screams of surprise and fear. Fear that something dreadful was happening in their church. Nope, no one was being harmed, no one was having a medical issue. Just three mischievous, idiotic teenagers.

After that, with my parents, the Barnetts, and Fr Fred, we were better off on the altar where he could keep an eye on us...

***

Meanwhile, back at the storage unit, Mara was laughing the hardest she had laughed in a long time. A very eye-opening statement. Her warm and friendly spirit is always swift to laugh. She laughs easily and often; most kind people do.

"Ayyy Dios MIO...this story is easily my favorite. I really love the stories that involve your brothers. This is the only one that also involves your father. "....... TAN bonito!!" The smile on her face told me she wanted another story. Personally, I never thought my suburban upbringing was anything but average, typical. I could tell we weren't leaving this storage unit until she heard one more story. But there was one more story worth telling. My favorite. Possibly the shortest story of all time, and my father is the story's protagonist.........I was 11 or 12 years old when my parents got the letter from my school..........." This one I know", Mara said with satisfaction. "It's the sex talk story."

***

8

The Talk

Chris had always been skilled at the art of strategic omission—never lying, never embellishing, but sidestepping the pain and embarrassment of his origin with a politician's grace. But this is a story Mara needed to hear.

***

I arrived home from school one day to find a letter on our kitchen table. I think I was 12. The letter just sat there. I knew it was from my school because I saw the familiar green and gold St Agnes School crest centered at the top of the letter. All I could think of was a letter from school. That could not be good. I was a high academic achiever, but still, the letter scared me. I was a very anxious kid who feared consequences and was ruled by them. The letter sat on the table for at least two days. I couldn't even summon the courage to read it. The strangest thing was that no one else seemed to be reading that letter either. What a weird family I come from. Finally, after another day or two had passed, the letter moved. It moved to a more centrally located position on the table. It was a big table. We had our meals there, and my mother paid the bills using it. My father did the daily crossword puzzle on that table. So, it was not unusual to see paper and general clutter on the table. There were always a few minutes of crossover in between my parents' work schedules.

*"Your father is getting home, so I'm going to get dressed before I go to work",
my mother said to me as she disappeared out of the kitchen. Finally, curiosity got
the best of me, and I read the letter. I couldn't take it anymore. I unfolded the letter
to see that the print was so brief, it was not even enough for an entire paragraph. I
regained my breath a little. I figured any bad news would come with pages and
pages of script. This was a paragraph only, and a small paragraph at that! The
letter, plainly said, underneath the green and gold St Agnes School crest, was a
matter-of-fact letter simply stating:*

Dear 6th Grade Parents:

**We are sending a notice home to all 6th-grade parents to inform you of
St. Agnes's official annual lecture on the topic of sexual education. 6th-
grade boys will meet as a group with Fr. Fred discussing issues to include:
sexual reproduction, sex and marriage, male anatomy, and venereal disease.
6th-grade girls will meet separately with Sister Rosa to discuss sexual
reproduction, the menstrual cycle, and teen pregnancy.**

*Oh my goodness, I wish I hadn't read that letter. It was way worse than I could ever
imagine. My parents were aware that we had our "sex talk". How embarrassing. I
didn't know how to react. I had about 30 seconds to hide because I knew questions
were coming from my parents, and even worse, they might even offer their own
takes on sexual reproduction and venereal disease. Good God, I didn't know which
was worse, the fact that we were taught about sex by celibate priests and nuns?
Or was it worse being taught by my parents? Both were probably equally trauma-
inducing. My parents were in perfect sync. Before the echo of the back door closing
diminished, my mother appeared to say this to me:*

"OK, Chris, I'm leaving for work now. Your father wants to have a talk with you."

*I turned my head toward my father just in time to see him pick up that letter from
the table. My heart raced, "OH MY GOD!!!" ....I thought to myself. I also thought
to myself," Didn't he read the letter in his hand....we had that talk with Fr. Fred*

TODAY!!!!", I have to listen to this again? My dear old dad was in worse shape than I was. I realized this, seeing him prepare himself for the sex talk with his youngest son, and then it happened. He spoke; he asked me:

"So, did they talk to you at school today about sex?". To that, my reply was this: "Yes". My dad's follow-up question was, "The priest, what's his name, Fr. Fred? He talked to you?"

"Yes" was my reply. My dear old dad thought for a moment and then added, "Do you have any questions?". Without hesitation, my reply was a staunch, "Nope," and to that, my father, the one-time professional boxer, replied, "OK, good." ... And that was my sex talk. ....

***

For the first time in this entire odyssey through my childhood, Mara was silent. Maybe stunned silence would have been a better description. For the first time that day, I led the laughter. Mara had no words for my description of my sex education. Mara came from a family with a long history of working in the medical field. Her father was a psychologist in Caracas, Venezuela. She had uncles and cousins who were doctors. So, discussing the human body and all its wonders was not an uncomfortable topic in her upbringing. So, to say she was shocked at my sexual education would be an understatement.

"Kind of explains a lot, doesn't it?", I said to Mara in hopes of getting a laugh, or at least breaking the silence. I went on to say that my sex talk is in the Guinness Book of World Records for being the shortest sex talk in history. Mara was finally able to speak. "You learned about sex from a priest?.... AND you went to an all-boys school?" ....." I'll repeat it, it explains a lot, doesn't it?". To that, we both laughed longer and louder than we had all day. I thought deeply for a moment before I said to Mara. "What do you think if our roles were reversed?"......."Not just the different countries and cultures.....I wonder how I would have been had I been raised by your parents....and what you would have thought being raised by mine?". Mara thought very carefully and had this to add, "Bueno, creo que si hubiera aprendido sobre sexo con sacerdotes y monjas como tú... habría quedado embarazada a los 13 años... o habría evitado a todos los hombres del planeta.".........Which roughly translates to I would be traumatized for life!!.........

"Venereal disease?!!!!!", she added....."Yes...maybe they thought we were sailors?"

"CRAP! CRAP! CRAP CRAP!" Chris was panicking. At the exact moment Mara realized it was 5:25pm, it was too late to go to the courthouse. Trying to soothe her husband, Mara simply said. "We'll find the birth certificate."

***

9

Listo!

Chris and Mara noticed the light dimming in the old storage space. Time flew by without their awareness. The consequences of losing track of time may be severe. Chris worried that Mara could get deported. It likely would not happen, but with the American political climate being what it is in 2024, you can't assume anything. At the very least, it would mean a delay in the process and cost the couple even more money.

But on the other hand, it resulted in a lot of tears and laughter, sweetness and bitterness. There were good days and bad days. Mara showed more emotion than her spouse. She was thankful to finally have the chance to honestly know her husband. After all, they met after he had already lived 50 years' worth of experiences. She felt their bond strengthen because of that storage unit. At that moment, she felt closer to him than ever before. Shadows stretched across the dusty floor as the light faded in the old storage space. Side by side, Chris and Mara's eyes adjusted to the darkening sky. They were surrounded by silence, save for the mice.

Chris's emotions swelled as he thought of his time with Mara in this place. Time had seemingly vanished, replaced by a collection of memories. Together, they were amazed that the storage unit's limits had broadened their relationship, exploring Chris's history. As shadows grew in the small unit, they felt an unprecedented closeness. The smell of old boxes and forgotten memories surrounded them, isolating them in their own world. Mara held

Chris's hand, feeling his calloused skin. It was a physical reminder of his past life, which she was just beginning to discover.

"You know, today has shown me your growth," Mara told Chris. "I think these old photos brought down some of your walls that a few months or years ago you would not have allowed them to fall. In fact, maybe you would have put up more walls." Chris was happy to hear this.

The two of them could have spent hours and hours in that old storage unit, a forgotten repository of a life lived. As the couple, Chris and Mara, finally exited, ready to continue their Christmas vacation, a tangible and intangible weight settled upon them. There was a lot to unpack. Both mentally and physically, they loaded several of the boxes into their rented car, which held more than just forgotten possessions. Mentally, unpacking all those memories was a little more complicated than just opening up the cardboard boxes. Unpacking these time capsules and all their contents held evidence of a life well lived, Chris thought to himself. He ran a hand through his hair, a nostalgic smile playing on his lips. There were a lot of good people he had experienced along the way. Seeing those old pictures brought back those people, at least for an afternoon. He could almost smell the pine needles from Christmas trees past, hear the laughter of friends long gone, and feel the warmth of a forgotten embrace. Mara, his wife of several years, enjoyed re-living those moments with him. She watched as he sifted through the photographs and trinkets, his face morphing through a kaleidoscope of emotions. His friends, his loves, his teachers, his family. Everyone who walks this big blue marble has these people and experiences in their lives. No two paths are the same, like no two snowflakes are alike. Mara now received answers to many questions that she had about her husband's experiences. Explanations revealed what made him shy, why specific topics made him happy, and which memories brought him sadness. She now knew that making friends was hard for him, not because he was incapable, but because he held the past so dearly. As they drove away, the city lights blurring in the twilight, Mara felt a sudden urge to speak. She considered it, wishing to speak. "I now know why you don't have a desire for friends". Chris, eyes fixed on the road, turned slightly. "Yeahh?

Cuentame, tell me why". "In your life, you had friends that were really, really remarkable...and I think that you don't want to ever think about anyone ever attempting to replace them," She wanted to tell him. She almost did, for indeed, he could never replace those beautiful and impactful relationships with John Barnet or Coach Horton, the football coach who had shaped him into a man. Nor could he ever have another "first love," like Grace, the girl with the sun-kissed hair who had stolen his heart in high school. No, Coach Horton, the man who showed by example how a good man leads with actions. She also pondered how lucky her husband had been to have people like that in his life, people who had helped shape him into the man he was today. She learned that Chris wasn't absent from social graces, a thought that sometimes she believed. His shyness wasn't a failing, but a testament to the depth of his past relationships and the profound impact they had on him. She understood now that his heart was a carefully curated museum of memories, filled with treasures he held dear, and that the idea of replacing those treasures was simply unthinkable.

Chris turned to his wife and surprised her with what he said next. "Those people were great....all of them, I miss them every day, and a lot of what you say is true."

"But!!!!! All of them combined cannot ever approach the impact that you have on me...and always will... There is not one person or one thing in this world that I will ever love as much as I love you."

This is not a story of one person's nostalgia. It's a realistic love story that took a lifetime of separate life experiences, each one of which was critical for their individual and separate evolutions. Life experiences that prepared them perfectly for their love of one another and their lives together.

"You're a good egg, Charlie Brown," Chris said, looking puzzled. Just then, she picked up an old paperback book with the title, 'It's a Charlie Brown Christmas.' Mara was reading the faded writing on the inside cover. She deduced that it was her father's handwriting.

"My father bought those books for me and wrote that," Mara smiled and said. "I agree."

***

"MARA!!!!!!!!!!", Mira!!!" The couple searched every box but one. Outside the unit, propping up the door was a heavy box. Mara and Chris had forgotten about that box; it was labeled in black, thick magic marker: FAMILY DOCUMENTS.

Chris hurriedly opened the box to find it meticulously organized, each offspring with their own individually labeled binder. Chris opened the binder that bore his name. There it was, perfectly preserved with an official stamp above the typewritten line that stated in all caps Chris's full name. Chris was reading it out loud as if to legitimize his own existence.

"CHRISTOPHER PAUL....."

And before Chris could finish reading it, Mara queried, "You were born at 1:38 AM." Chris said, "It appears so, according to the birth certificate." Mara hugged her husband, and they both sighed in relief, knowing that meant the population of the US had just increased by one.one.

THE END

About the Author

About the Author

    Christopher Gaffney lives in Austin, Texas, where he teaches middle school and spends his days surrounded by curious minds, adolescent behavior, and stories waiting to be told. When he's not navigating the daily adventures of classroom life, he's writing fiction that explores the quiet corners of everyday experience — where humor, heart, and humanity meet.

    He believes every great story starts with a simple "what if?" and usually finishes with too much coffee — or yerba mate.

You can connect with me on:

🌐 https://guayoyopublishing.com

📘 https://www.facebook.com/gaffney.writes

Subscribe to my newsletter:

✉️ https://guayoyopublishing.com